Cat's PAJAMAS

Dale Mayer

CAT'S PAJAMAS: BROKEN PROTOCOLS 2
Beverly Dale Mayer
Valley Publishing Ltd.

ISBN-13: 978-1-773363-88-2
Print Edition

About This Book

The future—where protocols must never be broken—is a very dangerous place indeed...

To save herself and her new lover, Lani Summerland agrees to marry Liev Blackburn. If not for the fact that the two of them are pawns in a game with no rule book, this might be a good thing for both of them.

Liev can't believe how lucky he is. But someone is after Lani, and, until he finds out who that is, there can be no honeymoon bliss.

Lani is targeted with not a clue what the stalker wants. The bodies begin piling up behind them. Luckily, they're not alone in their fight for survival. Lani's talking, super-intelligent cat, Charming Marvin, intends to save the day and his mistress so he can get back to his own chosen bliss—a much-needed cat nap.

Books in This Series:

Cat's Meow

Cat's Pajamas

Cat's Cradle

Cat's Claus

Broken Protocols 1-4

Sign up to be notified of all Dale's releases here!

https://geni.us/DaleNews

Protocol 2:3:5. You will in no way use force to damage the life of another—particularly if those actions are to selfishly enhance your own.

CHAPTER 1

MARRIED? TO LIEV Blackburn? Just like that? Lani Summerland's sense of humor kicked in. How typical of her crazy life. She couldn't find a man on her own in her twenty-first-century world, but was already married after a couple days in the twenty-third century. That was some matchmaking trick.

And not by choice.

Well, technically that wasn't true. The marriage part was by choice. At least it seemed like a great idea at the time. All of five minutes ago.

Lani Summerland stared suspiciously at the odd-looking adornment on her finger. It looked like a ring. It didn't feel like one. In fact, it had almost no weight to it at all. And, given the size of the deep purple rock on top, she thought she'd have noticed. Even the metal was soft, comfortable to wear.

She held her fingers splayed wide and shifted her hand in the age-old movement of women ever since rings were invented.

"Is it all right?" Liev Blackburn, her new husband, and yet still a stranger in many ways, stepped a little closer to her. The clear glass cube, or what stood in for an elevator of this time period was almost normal—but there was no way she'd become accustomed to it as it disappeared into thin air when they arrived at their destination. Not to mention it didn't follow normal pathways or tracks. In fact, it went where it was ordered to go by an invisible technology all its own.

She flashed him a quick grin. "Sure. I'm just not used to wearing big rocks that appear to be made of nothing or that adjust automatically to any size."

"It's the new alloys," Milo, Liev's brainy younger brother, piped up. "Gold fell from grace when the shortage came about ninety years ago. This was the answer. It's no different than the clothing you are wearing. It adjusts naturally to the size of the wearer."

Well, that explained the perfect fitting clothing she wore that never constrained or tugged at her or pinched her skin. Amazing. "And the supersize rocks?" she asked, playing with the rock to make it twinkle in the light.

"Most are synthetic." Milo judged his brother in a joking manner. "But not this one."

She frowned, pretty sure that the rocks in her day came in a synthetic variation as well. But they still had weight.

Then she had no time to wonder as they arrived at their destination. Her heart beat faster as she realized this was it. "Now remember. Just smile," Liev said. "Hold out your arm when requested to do so, but don't say a word unless asked a question." He shoved his arm outward to demonstrate.

She imitated his actions.

With a nod, he said, "If anyone asks where you're from, tell them you're from Felonia, and you arrived a couple days ago."

"Felonia," she repeated dutifully, dread congealing into a nasty ball in her stomach at the thought of anyone speaking to her. "Are you sure I can't just go home?" And back to Charming Marvin, who was even now resting in the pod at Liev's place.

"I wish you could. But, after this, no one will question your presence or your absence in the future." Liev wrapped an arm around her shoulder and led her forward. From all appearances, he looked like the doting new bridegroom. She shivered inwardly at the remembered passion they'd shared. Now if only they could head off on a romantic honeymoon.

But apparently not. She managed a warm glowing smile. He was her lifeline right now. And had quickly become the love of her life.

And, for that, she'd even put up with his brother Milo. Whom she had yet to forgive for dragging her into this century. Using an amazingly advanced computer program, he'd gone back in time, snatched her up, and brought her here as a gift for his brother, Liev.

Talk about a mind-bender.

That he'd also brought Charming and had accidentally enhanced his communication abilities, which were originally intended for her, was beyond anything she could have imagined.

The cube disappeared, and Liev, his arm still wrapped around her, led her forward into a large room with a clerk standing at the ready. "Good morning. Lani Summerland Blackburn," Liev said, "Liev Blackburn, and Milo Blackburn reporting in as requested."

The clerk frowned. "Only your presence was requested. Not your brother." He glanced up, saw Lani, and his frown deepened. "Not your girlfriend."

Lani straightened in outrage. Liev squeezed her shoulders. "My wife and brother are here because everyone living in my house was requested to attend."

"Wife?" Now the clerk's frown deepened. He clicked madly away on his weird tablet computer. Lani couldn't help but be fascinated as the lights flashed and pages shifted in a wildly erratic pattern she suspected was anything but erratic. She'd always loved computers. She hoped that she'd learn how these worked soon.

"Why do I have no record of that? I should have been notified." His voice rose slightly.

Control freak much? Lani eased out a shaky breath, trying to appear natural. As if showing up before a futuristic Council to answer for something she had nothing to do with was completely normal. She'd wanted to bring Charming with her for comfort, but both brothers had shot down that idea instantly.

Charming hadn't liked the idea much either. "Nope, this is a human thing. I'm going to do the cat thing and sleep the time away. Have fun though and ta ta till later." And he'd walked away from them, head held high, his tail straight in the air and the tip flicking in their direction.

Even now she wanted to go back and hug him. He was her only link to her old life. Then he'd always been special to her. The two of them only had each other for years. Now it seemed their family had unexpectedly grown.

The clerk finally looked up and studied her. Whatever he saw made his lips curl. "Don't tell me. She's from the outer areas. From a fringe group."

Cutting words bubbled up on Lani's tongue, but she bit them back. She had no idea what the *outer areas* meant, but she didn't deserve to be treated as a lesser person because of it.

Liev nodded comfortably. "She is."

The clerk rolled his eyes. "Whatever. I'll put her down."

Liev nodded his thanks politely and led Lani into a huge chamber room where the ceiling appeared so high up she couldn't see the top. "Wait here. I shouldn't be long."

She reacted instinctively, reaching out to grab his hand. "Are you sure you can't sit here beside me?"

He leaned over and dropped a kiss on her forehead. "You'll be fine." He looked up and nodded his head at someone. "Here's my lawyer. Hahn Driscoll."

Lani turned as the stranger approached. He wore a uniquely tailored suit in glowing blue patterns. The styles might not have changed a lot, but the colors of today sure had. She smiled a polite greeting and shook his hand, charmed at the old-style greeting.

"Liev. Are you ready?"

Liev nodded. "I was just settling Lani here, where she'd be comfortable."

Hahn smiled at her, and damn if one of his teeth didn't wink out at her in the same color as his suit. Wow. Tooth jewelry. Her gaze widened, and her breath caught in the back of her throat. It was all she could do to not say something. Instead, she turned to look around her to see the room filling up. Several people took seats. She decided the best thing was to do the same. She watched one man sit down on a black pole that instantly widened to accommodate his butt.

Taking a deep breath, she promptly sat down on the closest pole, her breath whooshing out when it opened successfully into a seat to support her butt. Thank heavens. She took a shaky breath and smiled up at the brothers. "Go on. I'll be fine."

Milo gave her a weird finger salute she guesstimated meant something similar to *Right on* and turned and bounced forward. He'd certainly dressed up for the occasion, wearing a black-and-white striped skin suit. She shuddered at the jailbird look. It didn't matter how long she lived here; she would never wear a skin suit like that.

As if understanding her thoughts, Liev bent over and whispered, "You'd look better in that than he does." He kissed her cheek, winked at her, and walked away.

The lawyer, thankfully not sporting painted-on skin pants, waited a few steps ahead for Liev to catch up. Heads bent deep in discussion, they strode out of the room.

And left her alone.

LEAVING LANI IN the waiting room was one of the hardest things Liev had ever done. She knew no one, knew nothing about the world she found herself in, or the pitfalls that awaited her every time she opened her mouth to speak. But he had no choice. He quickened his pace to catch up to Milo, who was strolling on ahead. His brother's flagrant disregard for the rules had put them in this situation. Only Liev had compounded the situation by using his friend's healing pod to help repair the damage done to Lani and Charming from time-traveling.

Liev could only hope that his friend's attempt to destroy the pod Liev had used to heal Lani in would make today's Council visit more of a maintenance checkup than an actual investigation. He'd had his lawyer meet them here just in case, but Liev hadn't had time to brief Hahn.

The legal fees that his company paid to keep Hahn's law firm available for times like this were exorbitant. As they were checked at the door and led into a smaller chamber, Liev spotted his old friend Stephen Cavendish on the Council dais. Relief swelled inside Liev. This might have started as a witch hunt, but it wouldn't end up that way. Stephen, young, only a junior Council member, was on Liev's side when it came to government meddling. And played the game well.

Liev smiled at his friend, relaxing even more when Stephen winked at him. This would be just fine.

Stephen opened the discussion. "I hear congratulations are in order, Liev?"

Liev beamed. "They are, indeed."

Milo bobbed at his side, his headset in his ear. He rarely spoke at these meetings. Probably just as well. What came out of his mouth usually didn't bode well for Liev or Milo.

In a genial let's-get-this-over-with-so-I-can-get-back-to-my-honeymoon tone of voice, Liev asked, "What is the problem that you needed to disturb me during my time of celebration?" He kept his face curious but amiable—at least he hoped it was. One sign of fear and these vultures would pounce.

"It's your friend Johan Strand," said one of the senior Council members. "He's wanted by the Council. When his request to appear was ignored, a team was sent to retrieve him. Unfortunately he'd set up some self-detonation on several of his equipment centers. Suspicious behavior at best." Some of the Council members nodded. "As your residence is known to be associated with him, we requested everyone there to appear here for questioning."

That's not quite the way Liev understood events to have gone down, but it wouldn't be the first time that the Council had twisted things to suit themselves. "First, Johan is an acquaintance, not a friend," Liev said in a what-has-this-got-to-do-with-me voice. "Second, I don't know anything about his equipment. Nor do I know where he is, if that is what you are looking to me for answers about." He stood tall and straight. "And my wife knows even less."

The Council stared at him. Even Stephen. Then again, Liev had always been good at playing the Council game.

Liev waited patiently. Ever since Milo had gotten them in hot water a year ago, whenever the Council wanted a question answered or needed to collect information, Liev and Milo were dragged down to appear in person. As if they couldn't lie or cheat their way through these sessions in person, like they might through a HoloKomp. He suspected that the Council ran illegal scans on every person who entered these rooms. Hence the reason for keeping Lani out. She might not pass the scans.

He needed the Council to find nothing wrong for a few more months. Then he would start asking them to back off before he involved the lawyers at a more in-depth level. As it was, today was one step from harassment. And Hahn had brought that up more than once.

But Liev needed to keep a low profile while Lani settled in. No one could take a closer look at her right now.

He couldn't imagine the shock of what she'd been put through. He didn't think he'd have handled it half as well as she had if he'd been in the same situation. In fact, he knew he wouldn't. He looked around, seeing Milo and his lawyer, … his extended family only a call away. He'd lose everything familiar and dear.

Just like Lani had.

For the first time, he had a little insight into all that she'd lost.

And how little he could do to make up for it. He'd done his best to protect her, but he could never replace everything.

"Liev?" Hahn nudged him. With a startled look at his old friend, he realized the Council was talking.

"We need to know any information," the elder Councilman, Carlson, said in a tone that demanded obedience. "Any names or locations that you may have heard Johan mention to track him down."

Liev frowned while he stopped to consider the request. "In truth, I'm not sure I ever heard him mention anyone or anyplace in particular. He was notorious for his parties, and serious talk didn't happen then, nor were any partygoers willing to engage in serious talk either."

"And yet, he mentioned the two of you going out for coffee after your last appearance here."

Liev's eyebrows shot up at the reminder. However,

he answered smoothly, "He did invite me, but the coffee never happened. He wanted to see his lawyers instead, so he asked for a rain check."

That, at least, was the truth. He suspected the Council members already knew what he'd done that day. A drone would have noted his and Johan's actions at the time and would have promptly submitted a report on both men, to be filed away for future reference.

The Council muttered among themselves for a long moment. "Your answers have been recorded. Should you have any further information to offer regarding the issue, please contact the office."

A different Council member spoke. "We notice that Milo has not added anything to the conversation."

Liev shrugged. "He has nothing to say. He had nothing to do with Johan."

"Not one of the regular partygoers?" Eyebrows shot sky-high, and amused twitters rippled through the Council members.

Milo was an anomaly to them. He lived in his own world and wouldn't have attended one of Johan's parties if Milo's life had depended on it. Milo's parties were always private with his other geek friends. Liev highly suspected they played more computer games than sex games when they were together. Milo's whole group was more active sexually in VR than in real life.

But that might also be his age or his perspective on other people. Milo was light-years ahead of others. While normal people looked into their coffee cups, wondering at the pretty pattern the cream made as it was poured, Milo had already analyzed its composition, calories, health detriments, and health benefits for everyone in the damn room, as well as who could tolerate that level of fat and who should be running in the opposite direction.

No one was like his brother.

Councilman Carlson said, "And the other occupant in your residence?"

"My wife, Lani?" Liev hated the way Carlson spoke about Lani. "You know her name is Lani. She isn't an occupant." She was so much more, but in their arrogance, they tried to dehumanize her that way.

"Is she here?" The speaker ignored Liev's comment, choosing instead to stare at him in a cold manner.

"She is waiting in the outer chamber." Liev curled his upper lip, his tone even but hard. "I speak on her behalf. All documents have been filed as per protocol."

After a moment where the men clicked away on their comps to verify his statement, the men nodded. Stephen smiled at Liev as they were dismissed.

Liev promptly turned and silently let his breath *whoosh* out. So they'd skated by safely again.

But for how much longer?

He pushed Milo ahead of him as they walked out. Now to collect Lani and get her home, safe and sound.

As he walked back into the anteroom, she no longer sat where he'd left her.

In fact, he saw no sign of her. "Shit."

CHAPTER 2

LANI SAT IN silence, watching in wonderment as the kaleidoscope of people walked by. Just like in her time, she saw a mix of races and ethnic groups. Skin appeared to come in a few more colors, like a light mauve, teal, and copper shades. She didn't know if those were medical enhancements, cosmetic changes, or something genetic. The copper-toned skins were beautiful, but the purple and pink ones were fascinating. Hair was another anomaly. It appeared as if anything went here. Colors from glittery black to Milo's wild green appeared on men in business clothing, similar to what Liev's lawyer wore.

The female in her was fascinated and a little jealous of the women here. Every color from the rainbow was represented—plus some she swore she'd never seen before. The skirts appeared to shift and almost wrap around the women's legs, as if it were some kind of intelligent material. And maybe it was. The fashions were unlike anything she'd seen before. It wasn't like old styles coming back around again. Instead, this time period had made huge leaps in terms of fashion sense. She glanced at her own interesting clothing, realizing she did fit in, but likely with a younger group than those she saw here.

Another thing that caught her gaze was the lack of purses or bags or even briefcases. How could that be? Everyone had to carry something.

Odd.

How did they carry laptops, tablets, or whatever the modern version was? Where did women put their makeup?

As she pondered life in this century, a beautiful businesswoman sat down beside her. Lani started. Dressed with severely coiffed hair in an almost purple-black one-piece skin suit, very little was left to the imagination. Lani stared. The woman's eyes were a deep emerald green. And her smile was nothing like anyone's she'd seen before.

"Hi, Lani."

Lani shrank back. Her tentative smile dropped away in shock. How did this woman know her?

"I'm Gina Stewart. Hahn is my law partner," the woman said reassuringly. "Our law firm represents Liev and Milo," she added.

Relief caused some of the tension to slip away. "Oh, they've all gone into that room." Lani motioned behind her.

The woman nodded. "That's normal." She paused, studying Lani's face intently. "But there's nothing normal about you, is there?"

Lani's gaze widened, her stomach sinking. "Pardon?"

"Oh, come on. That innocent-lost-girl look might work on Liev, but I know better." She settled more comfortably, but her sharp gaze never left Lani. Studying, probing, as if trying to figure out something. "You managed to marry one of the most eligible bachelors around. It's not as if I can do anything about that." Her smile turned glacial. "At least not right now."

Lani stared. She waited for the woman to say more. If Lani wasn't careful, this was a conversation guaranteed to get her into trouble. Like, what the hell? Was this woman jealous? Had she and Liev had a previous relationship? Her last comment sounded almost threatening. Too bad women hadn't changed with the times. Ambitious *cats* had existed in her century too.

When the other woman didn't speak again, Lani plastered a cool, confident smile on her face and said, "I'm sorry. I don't understand."

The other woman snorted and sat back, an irritated edge to her features. "Right. Fine. Be that way if you want." She looked around at the crowd. "Hopefully the men will be done soon, and we can leave."

Lani murmured something unintelligible. She was still struggling with her reaction. Relief and worry had taken over her bloodstream, and a headache like she'd never had before was building quickly. Too quickly. Where was a healing pod when she needed one?

"Are you all right?"

"I'm fine. Just a bit of a headache is all."

That brought the other woman's head around, her sharp gaze locking on Lani's face. "Why the devil would you allow one of those? Liev really fell for this back-to-natural stuff, huh? Never thought he'd be such a dupe." Gina snickered and stood. "Later."

And she walked away.

And what was that about *all natural*? Had people managed to do away with headaches completely here? But in a non-natural way? How confusing. More questions to ask Liev.

Lani was left to mull over Gina's words, her gaze on the woman's retreating back, when Gina just … disappeared. No cube surrounded her, nothing. She was there one moment, then gone the next.

Lani stared at the spot Gina had disappeared from to see a series of circles on the floor. She couldn't help thinking of the *Star Trek* movies from her day and the transporter system. Was that possible here? Or was this system even more advanced?

Other circles were on the floor, with people stepping in and out just as suddenly as they arrived and left. She hadn't noticed them before, the people traveling in such a way or that odd circle system. But where were they going to and coming from?

And how did they not crash into each other in transit?

She got shivers just thinking about it. What kind of a world had she found herself in? Her headache grew. She wished Liev was done. All she wanted was to be back home, safe in the healing pod with Charming.

And damned if her wrist didn't start to flash weird colors right then. Flustered, she dropped her arms into her lap and slapped her right hand over the lights. But they flashed brightly between her fingers. She had no idea what any of it meant. Neither had she seen anyone else's wrist start a light show.

Even as she thought that, it seemed as if everyone suddenly noticed her. Plain Jane Lani was getting way too much attention than was good for her. She tried to hide the bright lights against her belly but nothing seemed to do the job.

She searched behind her, desperately hoping for Liev or Milo to show up.

There was no sign of either of them.

Suddenly her arm was grabbed, and she was jerked up and out of her chair and pushed toward one of those weird circles. *Gina Stewart.*

"You're coming with me," the older woman snapped as she pushed Lani forward.

Lani stumbled and would have fallen but if not for Gina's grasp on her arm. "What are you doing?"

"Shut up."

Lani pulled back and managed to get free of Gina.

Gina snorted, gave Lani a short shove, and … the room disappeared.

Oh, no. Lani could hardly swallow. Her throat convulsed, and it was all she could do to keep the food in her stomach. She didn't know what had happened, but it hurt like hell.

"Jesus, what is wrong with you?" The disgust in Gina's voice had the effect of pushing the nausea up a notch, sending Lani almost to her knees.

"I'm sick," Lani whispered, bending over and trying to take deep breaths. "Where is Liev?"

"They're almost done. If you throw up in my office, I'm charging Liev for the damages."

"It wouldn't be in your office if you hadn't shoved me in here," Lani snapped with as much backbone as she could muster, helping regain her equilibrium. "Take me back to Liev."

Gina shook her head. "I don't get it. He actually married you? I can see partying for a day or two, but marriage?" She turned on her heel and opened her comp. "Hahn, I have Lani at the office."

She clicked off her comp. "Sit down, for heaven's sake. They should be here soon."

Shudders rippled down Lani's spine. She cast a quick glance around the gleaming iridescent room. There had to be something to sit on—just not something she recognized as a chair. "I'll stand," she said quietly.

That only earned her another disgusted look. "Whatever." Gina walked out of the room, leaving Lani alone.

Thank God.

A window was open on the far side. Not trusting that she was truly alone or that she wasn't being recorded in some way, she walked over to the window, schooled her features, and looked out. Another traffic scene. This time she studied the vehicles and the pattern of controlled pandemonium. She didn't think she'd ever drive in this lifetime. The sheer speed of the chaos outside the window shook her. That she didn't know the rules of the road was one thing but she didn't think she'd ever be comfortable enough to follow whatever passed for driving rules here.

This place was just too … *out there* for her.

And where the hell were Liev and Milo? They shouldn't have left her alone. At least not for this long. She understood on one level, but on another … how was she to know about the Ginas of his world or the weird circles on the floor and the nonexistent furniture she was supposed to sit on? She hadn't had a chance to do or see or learn anything. She'd been concerned with healing enough to just walk.

She heard an odd *whoosh* in the center of the room.

She spun around, her hand going to her chest. Now what?

LIEV TURNED IN a slow circle, his gaze darting from side to side. "Come on, Lani. Where are you?"

Milo stared at him. "What did you say?"

"Where's Lani?" Liev muttered softly.

Milo's gaze widened in horror, and he spun around.

And continued to spin in a slow movement as he searched the room a second time.

"Maybe she had to go to the washroom," he suggested.

Hahn approached the two of them. "I'll file a motion when I get back to the office to have any further Council meetings done by comp. It's ridiculous that we have to continue to show up in person to answer a few questions."

Liev pulled his attention back to look at Hahn. "Good. Please do that. And thanks for your help there." He watched as his lawyer walked away, the blue of his suit shimmering in the brilliantly colored crowd.

As soon as he was out of sight, Liev spun to find Milo working on his comp. "Tell me that you found her."

"There's no sign of her anywhere." Milo swore under his breath before sucking it in sharply. "Wait. Incoming."

Where the hell could Lani have gone? Liev lifted his shoulders. "Incoming what?"

Milo gasped, then choked. "Incoming message. From Charming Marvin?"

Liev turned so he could see Charming's feline face over Milo's shoulder. "Lani is in trouble. Tracking … now on."

"What the hell?" His words, even voiced low, caught the attention of curious passersby. Damn. The place was crowded. Still, their curiosity was a good reminder that anything they did and said was likely being recorded.

"Yeah, he's good." Milo clicked a few more buttons. "Got her. She's at Hahn's office."

"How the hell …" Liev raced to the ports.

"Gina took her there," Milo called out, running behind him.

He stepped into the port and appeared at Gina's office, Milo right behind him.

And there was Lani.

She stared at him in shock. When she realized he was here in person, she raced toward him. He caught her in his arms and hugged her tightly. "It's okay," he murmured. "I'm here."

She couldn't stop shaking or burrowing closer. Her arms locked around his waist and wouldn't let go. He held her close and continued to whisper comforting things in her ear. She was stiff and unyielding— terrified. He could just imagine … and hugged her closer.

"As you can see, she's fine," Gina snapped. "Lord, all this fuss over nothing."

Milo came to Lani's rescue first. "Really? You remove someone from the Council offices without anyone's permission, including that of the woman you kidnapped, and you say it's *nothing?*"

At the word *kidnapping*, Gina gasped, and Lani burrowed deeper into Liev's embrace. "I did no such thing." Gina stormed closer, her perfect face twisting in fury. "Lani was attracting attention. What did you expect me to do?"

"In what way was she attracting attention?" Liev asked, trying to keep his own rage under control. Which was hard as Lani burrowed closer.

"She sat so damn still. So perfect. Like a statue." Gina snorted, disgust threading her voice. "She didn't move, no comp, no nothing. Just an oddness that stood out." She shrugged. "Then her ID started to flash. It was too close to the Missing Person's Alert. Like, really?" Gina rolled her eyes. "I had to stop her from making a spectacle of herself."

"So because she wasn't *you*, you figured she was odd." Milo mimicked her voice so perfectly that Liev had to bite back a grin. "And her ID could flash for any number of reasons."

"It wasn't so much that it flashed, it was the look of shock, horror, and confusion on her face that was so ridiculous." Gina glared at them. "She was fine when I first saw her. So I left her alone. Only after I returned did I realize she was causing such a commotion."

Milo narrowed his eyes. "And you couldn't leave it alone. Not because she was garnering attention, but because *you* weren't. For some reason, Liev married *her*, not you. *She* had him. You didn't. It was all about jealousy, wasn't it?" Milo snapped forward from his sixteen-year-old mental self with a wisdom beyond his years. "Liev partied with you, and you wanted more. He didn't. Next thing you know, he shows up with this natural girl and is married to her."

Gina's voice turned cutting. "Go back to bed, Milo. It's a little late for you to be up, isn't it?"

Lani lifted her head from Liev's chest and, in low tones, asked, "Can we go home now?"

He hugged her gently. To the others, he said, "You two can stay and fight if you want. I'm taking her back. She's been sick and needs rest."

"She could get that fixed. Playing on your sympathies, you know." Gina raised both hands in frustration. "Whatever." And she strode out of the room again.

Milo glared at her receding back. "Bitch."

Lani giggled. "Glad to hear that word is still used nowadays."

"Especially nowadays," Milo said with a smile. "Let's go home."

"Yes, please. By the way," she said, "how did you know I was here? Gina left a message on Hahn's comp, or whatever that thing is, but I didn't see her call you two."

"That's because she didn't," Liev said, loosening his arms and turning her gently, nudging her from the room.

Milo bounced on his heels to his toes. "You aren't going to believe what did happen."

She twisted slightly to look him in the face. Liev kept her walking forward. "Why? What happened?" She looked up at Liev. "Hahn called you?"

Milo shook his head, almost dancing with glee now.

Liev gave a low and deep rumble of a laugh. "Charming Marvin told us."

She came to a dead stop and stared at him. "What? Really?"

They both nodded.

Her sense of humor kicked in, and she giggled.

Liev grabbed her into his arms for a hug, stepped into the same circle Lani had popped out of earlier, and led her out into the Council anteroom within seconds. Her joy was a light in his life. She had to be feeling rough enough without enduring the cutting edge of Gina's tongue, but it hadn't gotten her down. Lani was a survivor.

Gina had been a mistake years ago. Liev should never have hooked up with her. After she'd joined his lawyer's firm, their first business meeting had been slightly uncomfortable, but then he'd promptly forgotten about her and the weekend party. An easy thing to do.

To think she'd gone after Lani, regardless of her motives, concerned him. She'd said it was to protect him, to protect Lani, but there'd been no need to remove Lani from where he'd left her. And, if Gina *had* said something to Hahn, why hadn't his lawyer said something to Liev?

Liev mulled it over, not liking where his thoughts were taking him. An innocent miscommunication? Or something more sinister?

Milo's comp beeped again. The three were back in

the Council anteroom, where Lani had originally been waiting for them. He led them back out through security. On the other side, Milo stopped and tugged Lani toward him. "Could you please look into my comm?"

She shot him a startled look. "What?'

He held out his arm, and the tiny screen flashed in front of her. Obediently she stared into the comp. Immediately it flashed. Then the screen cleared, and Charming's flat face filled the screen. Charming gave her a huge cat grin.

She gasped in joy. "Oh, please, let's go home."

"Right now." Liev stepped into the elevator cube which appeared to morph into a tube at some odd times. The other two crowded close to him. The trip back was fast and efficient. Lani appeared to have relaxed about their traveling system, and that was good. It was just one of many things she'd have to learn to do on her own. Just as Liev had other things to learn. Like how to deal with a talking cat who could send an alarm about Lani. What Liev didn't understand was how Charming knew Lani was in trouble in the first place.

It would be the first thing he'd ask the talking feline.

CHAPTER 3

"HER VITALS HAD gone off the chart," Charming explained, in between licking the nutrient-rich cream off the plate, his tongue making little *snick, snick* sounds. "I saw a flashing button labeled Scan, so I pressed it and didn't like the results." He shrugged. "It was obvious she was upset. There were too many variables to pinpoint the reason, so I figured you should be the one to deal with it."

Charming lifted his head, pink cream dotting the fluff of orange fur sticking out in a tall cloud around his face, and asked Lani, "What was the problem anyway?"

"Oh, nothing," she said tiredly. "Just an old girl-friend of Liev's who decided to kidnap me."

Charming spluttered, sending pink cream all over the table. "What?" He lifted his head to stare at her, his shock widening his gaze.

Relieved to be home, her fear slowly subsiding now that she was safe and back with Liev, she gestured in Liev's direction. "He'll give you the details."

Charming turned to face Liev. When he didn't jump in with an explanation, Charming stalked across the table closest to where Liev stood and glared at him.

"Liev, explain."

The look on Liev's face made Lani choke back a giggle. He looked like he'd swallowed a sour candy.

"What's the matter, Liev? Not used to explaining yourself, especially to a cat?" she murmured as she walked past him to stare out the window. He gave a snort, but she ignored him, choosing to study the outside world again, this time with a jaundiced eye.

Behind her, she heard Liev explain about the short relationship he'd had with Gina a long time ago, shortly after she had joined the firm, working for Liev's lawyer. Damn, Lani knew that whatever happened in Liev's life before her arrival should have nothing to do with her. But somehow her rules didn't sound like they'd apply in this case. Gina wouldn't let them.

"Why would she do this to Lani?" Charming asked.

"I don't know," Liev admitted. "It makes no sense."

"Yes, it does," Milo piped up, adding, "She's jealous. She heard about your marriage just this morning, as did everyone else, and reacted badly. An opportunity presented itself, and she snatched it."

Lani winced. That woman's damn superior tone had said more about Gina than Lani cared to know. She *was* a bitch. If she'd dated Liev, that was one thing, but, according to Milo, Liev had had an affair with her. At least that's what Lani thought *partied* meant. Like, really? That was what he considered his type?

If the other women of this century were the same as the barracuda lawyer, no wonder Liev hadn't yet hooked up with anyone permanently. She wouldn't have either. Maybe Milo had done Liev a favor in bringing Lani here.

"But she didn't do anything other than take Lani to her office," said Liev, his frustration and temper showing in his voice. "It's not as if she hurt her or demanded money. It's more like she wanted to check Lani out for some reason."

"She kept calling me *natural* or something like that." Lani spun around to look at the men. "What does that mean?"

"Ha." Milo laughed. "Everyone is improved these days. Babies are born with the preferred genetic markers, so there is no illness anymore … or very little. Brainpower can be chosen. Looks. Things like that. But it's the parents' choice of course. When the child grows up, they can also choose their own enhancements. Similar to cosmetic surgery from your day," Milo added. "Every society has fringe groups. Naturals are one of ours. People who eschew any non-natural improvements."

"So because I don't have any enhancements, I'm natural looking, so that's something to laugh at?" Lani asked. "Really?"

Charming snorted. "Some of us don't need enhancements."

Liev smiled and reached out to scratch Charming under the neck. Charming's eyes crossed with pleasure. "Not all enhancements work or are an improvement.

Many times the person looked better before the enhancement. But there will always be those who have to push the edge."

"And, Milo," Lani asked, "are you one of those genetically chosen brains?"

He smirked. "I am that and so much more. Something different happened with me, and I ended up with more than expected."

"Meaning, he was likely a genius naturally," Liev said. "By genetically choosing more intelligence, our parents had no idea they'd get someone at the far end of that spectrum."

"Did they understand his nature before they passed away?"

Liev nodded. "Yes, they did. Milo could read before his second birthday and could solve calculus problems before his fourth. He hasn't stopped since."

"And you," Lani said gently, "how do you feel knowing that your parents gave Milo all those brains, but they didn't give them to you? Presumably it was an option."

"One can ask for genetic markers to be enhanced, but no one can guarantee the results. They chose different markers for me." He shrugged. "And I'm happy with who I am."

He didn't mention what the other genetic markers were and left Lani trying to guess. He'd tell her when he was ready.

She turned back to the window. What kind of

world could already determine what their children would be like before they were even born? "Where is Mother Nature in all this?" she murmured. "Does she still have a role to play?"

"That's the thing about Milo. If you take ten different fetuses with all the same genetic markers like his, you won't get ten Milos. Mother Nature still rules."

That made her feel better. She hated to think that everyone was now preordained to be a specific way.

And she refused to believe this was an improvement over the rules of her old society. She couldn't argue that she'd love to be better at some things. Speed-reading was an example. She'd wanted to go back to school, had just been accepted into an IT Security program before Milo so rudely yanked her out of her life. Now that little training program would be laughable to what she'd need to learn for a successful life here.

She stopped in her tracks. Was it possible? She turned slowly, realizing even Charming was better suited to life here, due in part to his enhancements. Were there some enhancements that would help her to adapt, to learn what she needed to know to thrive here?

"Is there something you can do to enhance me too?" she asked slowly, studying their faces. "Some way for me to learn what I need to know about your society? About how to live here safely. About your government. Your monetary system. There's so much I don't know. Is it possible to get some kind of, ... I don't know, ... microchip downloaded to my brain or something?"

Milo stared at her in fascination. "Wow. That would be so cool."

And she realized there wasn't that possibility for her. She sighed. "Damn. If I could speed-read or something, I could whip through all the schooling of your times until I caught up with my age group. Surely I could understand how this time period functions by the end of that."

"That's not a bad idea." Liev looked at her in surprise. "Milo, you can set her up with a VR system that will walk her through the lower learning levels."

"No one does grade school anymore," Milo said in surprise. "What good will that do?"

"It'll be the little things that trip me up," Lani explained. "Things that every child will know."

"But they are born with most of that knowledge. Or they already have it by the age of five."

"So how can I get the same knowledge then? You didn't end up enhancing me. You enhanced my cat."

"Hey, how was I to know you'd bring a critter with you?" Milo protested. "I'm not taking the blame for that."

"No one is blaming you," Charming said with a sniff. "Personally, I like it."

"You would," muttered Lani. She wanted to run back into the pod and forget about this place. Maybe she'd wake up in the morning, and this nightmare would be over. But she'd asked for that before, and it hadn't happened yet.

"I think Milo can help you," Liev said calmly. "We do have virtual reality learning modules. He also has boosters to help you learn faster and to retain what you learn. It won't be so bad. We can get you through most of the basics in a few weeks."

Weeks? With a tired nod, she walked back to the small room that had the pod. Fully dressed, she climbed inside and closed her eyes. Hot tears threatened to pour out. Instantly the pod hummed as it worked to heal her. Only there was no healing this.

How did one heal a lack of self-confidence, a feeling of being overwhelmed, and a knowledge that she would always be the stupid relative from the fringe society in which others thrived?

She closed her eyes, curled up in a fetal position, and sobbed.

LIEV REACHED OUT a hand as Lani walked past. She didn't see him, and his hand dropped away. He didn't know how to help her.

As she disappeared around the corner, he was afraid he'd seen her shoulders shake. She'd had an incredibly trying couple of days.

"Well, go fix it." Charming gave him a flat stare that made Liev pause.

"And how would you like me to do that?" he asked.

Charming's gaze never blinked. "How about the

same way you fixed it last time?"

And, damn, if heat didn't climb up Liev's neck as he realized just how much Charming understood.

"How did you fix it last time, bro?" Milo asked, walking closer, as if that would help him understand the solution.

Liev groaned silently. "Never mind." He spun on his heels and hurried after Lani. He wished he could fix it like last time, but somehow he knew it wouldn't be that easy. Not now that Gina had become involved. He'd avoided her after that one weekend because she'd become possessive. Meddlesome. Unlike Lani, Gina was the kind to push herself into situations where she wasn't wanted. And laugh while doing so. But her actions today? … He'd have to contact her and sort it out. And he also needed to talk to Hahn as to why he hadn't passed on the message about Lani's whereabouts. Not for the first time, he wondered at the loyalty of those he employed.

Lani's subdued sobs reached him in the hallway. Shit.

He bowed his head. He had to stop putting her in situations where she ended up in tears. They were obviously her coping mechanism. But how sad that she ended up crying as often as she did right now.

He walked to the pod and opened the lid. He sat down at the end and tugged her into his arms so he could look into her teary eyes. "First, I'm sorry you had to go to the Council this morning."

She blinked those wet baby blues at him.

"Second, I'm even sorrier that you had to deal with Gina this morning. I'll get to the bottom of what she was up to. I promise."

She blinked several times.

He waited curiously. When she didn't say anything, he continued, "And, as for helping you to learn the world around you, I'll take off the next few days from work to go over the basics with you. Then we can hook you up to an education system and go through the lower levels first. Milo will be able to help you learn faster."

"*Faster?*" she asked cautiously, a glint of curiosity peeking through the waterworks.

Thank heavens. "Yes, we have modules you can listen to while you're asleep, and you should assimilate the information at a rapid rate."

Her curiosity turned to excitement. "Now that would help."

He smiled. "I won't leave you in the dark about my world. I should have taken a few minutes earlier to make you understand the ports. They are in all major centers, like the Council chambers. As long as the circle is empty when you step into one, you are tagged." He lifted her wrist as a reminder of her implanted tag. "Then the ports take you home or to work. If someone is already in transit, the arrival is delayed to sequence landings in the proper order. Ports read your tags automatically."

"But I didn't go to either of those places."

"No. Gina's tags were coded for her office and the Council, as part of her work. Not everyone can use them all the time." He paused, wondering how to clarify it. "The Council is an important part of the system and requires easy access for people in law enforcement. People working in police stations, lawyer's offices, the jail system, at the parole board, and others in some related fields must have access, so they can bring someone with them. They have an override. So, even if you wanted to go home, because Gina was there in an official capacity, she would have automatically overruled you—unless you knew how to change the coding to come home."

"Then learning how to change the coding is what I want to learn first."

He paused. "That's not a bad idea. You were in computers before, weren't you?"

She shrugged. "Only in a small way. And nothing like your computers of today."

"No, but it shows an aptitude. And we can build on that."

Without realizing it, he'd shifted her position so she was in his lap, cuddling her against his chest. He dropped his chin to rest on the top of her head. "We will make this work."

"So many pitfalls are out there," she muttered, but her tone was softer, more relaxed.

"There are, but we can teach you."

"And Gina, is she likely to be someone I have to see a lot?" She pulled away slightly from Liev, as if withdrawing into herself.

He tugged her back. No way would he let her go. Or give her a chance to squeeze more distance between them. He dropped a kiss on her forehead.

She stiffened slightly, then melted. She wasn't completely comfortable in his arms, but she wasn't against it.

He, personally, didn't think he could get enough.

CHAPTER 4

LANI HATED IT when she behaved badly. Crying was getting to be a habit, and she had to stop it. She wasn't weak, just overwhelmed. As in, she'd hit the wall.

Sure, she'd had a shock. Sure, she'd been scared, but she also knew people, and this wouldn't be the last time she came up against someone who didn't like her presence in Liev's life. The fact that he'd married her would add to that disgruntlement and disbelief from other women.

Gina had wanted more from Liev than he'd been willing to give—she likely still did. Lani didn't know what had been on Gina's mind this morning, but Lani would just as soon avoid seeing Gina again. "I don't get how Charming sent you a warning. Even if he did get the enhancement. And I hate thinking he is superior to me now." She wasn't sure how to reconcile the amazement and jealousy she felt over that bit. "How did he alert you?" she asked Liev.

"He called Milo on the house comp. We had just returned to the room where we left you, and, with Charming's info, Milo could track you easily. Because of Charming, your wrist tag went crazy. He noticed your vitals were rising, after we left you alone so he ran a scan that set off your wrist tag. He called us after that. I have no idea how he knew to do that, but he did somehow."

She didn't know what to think. "So Charming didn't know where I'd gone?"

"Not really. He only knew that you'd moved and that your vitals had gone *off the chart*." Liev grinned. "To put it mildly."

"Yeah, the meeting with Gina wasn't exactly a warm bonding experience."

He laughed. "Gina was never into warm or bonding. She's into what's in it for her."

"Nice. *Not*," Lani said. "You have interesting choices in women."

"Not my choice," he said almost absently.

"What?" She froze and gave him a wide-eyed stare. "You mean, Milo chose her for you too?"

He started. Then a rumble started deep inside his chest as his laughter rolled freely. "No, he didn't," he gasped when he could. "Sorry. I meant to say that I met her at a weekend party a long time ago. I had nothing to do with her after that. She called many times, but I wouldn't go out with her. Never had any intention of doing so."

"Well, guess what? The silent treatment isn't working. Because you never said no, she's still working that angle, thinking that maybe this time you will say yes."

He glanced down at her in surprise. "This was years ago. She's not still interested."

"If she's not still interested, then she's happy to get a little revenge instead." Lani did understand women. And that was something in her experience that men never seemed to get. Rejection was a bitch. And some bitches never forgot.

"I'll make sure she stays away from you."

Lani wasn't so sure. "She's a lawyer and could make a lot of trouble for us if she chose to." Lani knew, to her regret, how some lawyers acted. Not all of them were the same, but Lawrence Blackburn, her former boyfriend in her time, and Liev's "blackhearted ancestor," as Liev had put it, had been bad enough to give her a warped perception of lawyers.

"No," Liev said with such surety that she started to relax. "She won't."

"Yeah, I hate to bother you two, but Hahn is calling, bro." Milo's voice filtered overhead from the built-in sound system. "You need to deal with this."

"Damn," Liev said. "You stay here in the pod, and I'll go talk to Hahn."

She tried to slide off his lap only to find herself being lifted, then laid down on the wide bed. He lowered the lid, clicked a few buttons, and walked away.

Immediately the pod started to hum again. Disappointed that he didn't kiss her goodbye, she rolled over and closed her eyes. Suddenly the pod opened again, and he stood there in front of her. With a heated look, he lowered his head and kissed her.

Heat licked down her spine, her toes curled, and her mouth surrendered to his onslaught.

Then he was gone.

She sighed happily, tucking up into a contented ball.

"Really? Do you have to moon around like that?" Charming said from the floor level. He jumped up and padded up toward her. The lid slowly closed over them.

She laughed. "*Moon?* I think they need to work on updating your vocabulary, Charming, for this particular century." She shuffled backward to give him more room, her hand instinctively reaching up to pet her best friend. "Thank you so much for telling the brothers where I was this morning. That was a horrible experience."

He leaned into her hand, rubbing his head against hers. "They shouldn't have taken you out there."

"I agree," she exclaimed, "but the Council's orders were explicit."

"*Hmm.*" He padded in a circle before curling into a ball. "I wonder why?"

She tilted her head to look at him closer. "Charming? What are you wondering about?'

He started to snore.

She frowned. "Are you just pretending to be asleep?"

"No." But he kept his eyes closed, and the snores kicked in again.

"Right." He might not be pretending at this point, but he was only one step away from making it a reality. She rolled over, giving the pod access to her back.

She could feel herself getting sleepy. Nothing like nerves, shock, and then recovering under soothing warmth to wear one out.

She closed her eyes and slept.

"HAHN, WHAT'S UP?" Liev stood in front of the Holo-Komp, trying to remain cool and collected when all he wanted to do was return and finish what he had started. Lani was warm, wet, and willing. And he was a newly-wed. He wanted to get back to his wife.

That thought brought a smile to his face.

"I don't understand the humor in this situation," Hahn said stiffly, his gaze hardening in the holographic image in front of the wall. "Glad you think this is all a farce."

Now what? "As I don't understand the situation, perhaps you could fill me in." He kept his voice cool, professional, and just on the edge of pissed. That was the thing about lawyers; they seemed to always forget who signed their paychecks. Hahn more than most.

"Gina quit the firm. She says she can't protect you and your new wife in any court scenario. She is citing irreconcilable differences between her and ..." Hahn looked down as if reading from a sheet of paper. "Lani."

Liev wanted to cheer. That was perfect if she quit. "I'm delighted to hear that. I can't say her behavior this morning was anything but one step short of criminal."

Hahn's eyebrows shot up, even as the look of anger receded slightly to be replaced by confusion. "What? Did I miss something?"

"I have a question for you that pertains to this morning's issue. Did you receive a communication from Gina, stating that Lani was with her in her office?"

Hahn frowned. "Not that I know of. Why? Wait. Gina's office? Why was Lani there?"

"Exactly what I'd like to know. Apparently Gina grabbed Lani's arm and shoved her into a port and took her directly to her office. She treated Lani like a criminal, offering no explanation for her actions. Lani was traumatized by the actions of a woman who is supposed to be helping me and mine." His voice gained a sharp edge at the end. "I hardly see that as appropriate behavior. I left explicit instructions for Lani to be in that seat when I returned. I don't care if you don't like my instructions, Hahn, but I do expect them to be carried out."

Hahn's face shifted from frustrated to startled to worried. "I have no idea what she was thinking. She said the girl was making a spectacle of herself, and she tried to calm her down. When that wasn't working, she went back to the office."

"*Spectacle?*" Liev said in an ominous tone. "In what way was Lani making a spectacle of herself?"

"I don't know honestly. Just that many people were staring at her. She's odd, you know," he said apologetically. "Different."

"*Natural* is the insult that Gina used." And now that he had a better idea of what Gina thought about Lani, he was delighted Gina was leaving the firm. Liev watched the rush of emotions slide across the face of a man who had worked for him for a long time.

"Liev." Milo worked on the big 3-D monitor in the kitchen beside Liev and just out of Hahn's sight. Milo was always on one of the many computers in the house. He'd been clicking like a madman for a few moments; then he punched a fist in the air.

"Look at this." He punched a couple more buttons, and suddenly the feed from this morning showed up on the HoloKomp, where both Liev and Hahn could watch.

All three men watched as Gina approached Lani, sitting quietly in the chair, oblivious to Gina's approach. After a short conversation, Gina checked her watch, glancing around at the crowd. The crowd moved past Lani, but in no way was she making a spectacle of herself.

Gina left. Then Lani's wrist flashed. It was apparent that she was trying to cover it up. Gina returned, said something, then she tugged Lani upward, almost dragging her to the ports. Gina pushed Lani into the closest one. Liev's gut clenched as he watched the shock and fear on Lani's face before she disappeared from the screen.

"Jesus." Hahn's shocked exclamation came through clearly before he managed to cover it. "I don't know what was on Gina's mind, but I will be speaking with her about this."

"And will she still be working for your firm after this?"

"I had planned on asking her to reconsider her resignation." At the sound coming out of Milo's mouth, Hahn winced. "She's very popular with our clients."

"*Male* clients," Milo said in disgust. "I bet she doesn't work with any female ones."

They both watched as surprise lit up Hahn's face, before his features twisted as he considered the issue. "You know what? I think you might be correct." His lips grimaced downward. "Let me talk to her."

"And get back to me with an answer. Then I can make my decision as to how I will proceed."

Before Hahn could respond, Liev disconnected the HoloKomp.

As the screen went black, Liev turned to Milo. "Send him a copy please, and keep that recording, in case we need it again."

"Done." He was busily tapping the flat counter screen, obviously searching for something. Liev watched his brother work. When Milo went on the hunt, there was no hiding anything from him. "What are you doing now?"

Rather than answering, Milo grabbed the corners of

a small window and stretched it enough for Liev to see Gina's office clearly. Then Milo switched the time clock, backing it up to when Lani should have arrived. Last, he clicked on the speakers.

Liev grinned. Milo had tapped into Gina's security feed.

After a weird popping sound, all of a sudden Lani arrived in the office. Scared and stumbling to maintain her balance—in more ways than one—she bent over suddenly, her face green.

They watched the next few minutes in silence until the two brothers arrived at the office after Charming had alerted them. At one point, Milo stopped the feed, enlarged it, and backed it up so they could replay the section when Gina sent a message to Hahn.

Lani was right, at least as far as she understood. Gina had left a communication for Hahn, but the name wasn't clearly audible. Was it for the same Hahn or a different one? Or was it a fake communication? A coded message? Liev lived in a world of corporate espionage. He didn't take anything at face value.

Milo voiced his doubts. "I wonder who she left that message for." He switched cameras and zoomed in on her wrist comp, found a series of numbers. None of them were Hahn's code. So she'd left a message for a different Hahn. Milo immediately started a search. Within seconds, he had a name.

Johan Strand.

Not Hahn Driscoll, Liev's attorney, not even another Hahn, but a Johan. Liev's old friend. One on the run himself. And one who was taking way too close an interest in Liev's affairs. With one of Liev's lawyers.

Was Johan a friend? Or not any longer? Had he ever been?

The one thing Liev knew about Johan, the man was an opportunist.

So what the hell was he up to now?

CHAPTER 5

LANI SURFACED TO a feel-good stretch with warmth bathing down on her. These pods were something. She was so happy to be in here. Registered or unregistered, the pod was a huge help, and she was grateful. She could just imagine those with arthritis lying here after a long day and feeling the healing rays beat down on their swollen joints. Or those with physical jobs. It used to be that having a Jacuzzi tub was the best way to end the day, but with one of these babies? … Wow.

Then she had to wonder if physical work was done in this century anymore. Did labor jobs exist? And that took her to another form of labor. Did women still go through labor, or did they give birth in a pod? Or did they go to sleep and wake up with a newborn? She laughed. Most likely there was no such thing as pregnancy or labor. Kids were probably created in test tubes now.

"Did that mean computerized nannies as well? Day-care dummies? Kindergarten komputers?" She laughed. "Better not be that way. Right, Charming?"

"A cat computer would be good," he murmured sleepily. "A custom chef for cats would also work. How about a computerized cat scratcher? I do need someone to take care of me when you're not here."

"Ha." She smirked. "I am not going anywhere ever again."

"Little do you know."

She sat up, pushing the pod lid out of her way so she could slide her legs over the side. She stopped to look down at Charming, now sprawled across the bed, taking up her spot. He was seriously relaxed. "Are you feeling better now? Back to normal?"

He lifted his head to look at her. "Still tired but better." And he dropped his head down.

As long as he wasn't screaming for food anymore, they were good. She could use some of that wonderful coffee though. She walked slowly from the pod, happy when the room looked normal and the walls stayed straight. She used the bathroom, then walked into the kitchen. And stopped.

"Holy crap," she cried out.

Charming must have heard her, for he raced down the hall toward her. "What?"

They both stared.

The countertop had been converted to some kind of large computer screen, and both brothers were bent over it, searching through various screen loads that, at the touch of their fingers, moved and shifted, changing form and colors. Fascinated, she walked forward, her gaze on the computer screen loads as they rippled past. Charming followed at her side, then jumped into a nearby chair to get a better view, his gaze locked on the colors and images as they winked on and off, mesmerized.

"What is this?" Lani asked.

"A computer." Milo looked at her in surprise. "Surely you've seen one of these?"

"I've seen many but nothing like this." She searched the massive countertop for something recognizable in terms of commands. She found none. Neither was there a keyboard. She watched pictures of offices and buildings flash by. "What are you looking for?"

"Who, not what," Milo answered absentmindedly. "Johan."

"Your friend? Why?"

Liev snaked an arm around her waist and tugged her closer. Smiling, she wrapped her arms around his waist and snuggled in. "He's the one Gina contacted in the lawyer's office. It was Johan, not Hahn."

She frowned. "Are you sure?"

"Very. We watched the numbers as she coded them on her personal comp device. We managed to get a recording. It was Johan."

She shook her head. "You guys have a feed of that room from that specific time?"

"Milo found it."

Of course Milo did. She wondered what the Council would say if they knew he appeared to go wherever he wanted to electronically, and could retrieve any information he wanted. Nothing good, she was sure.

"Milo is on our side, and that's a good thing," Liev murmured.

"I'll say." She watched the screens flash by. Up on top of the screen was some kind of counter. She didn't understand, but it appeared to be connected to the flashes.

Suddenly she heard a *beep*, and a single window surfaced and flashed.

Liev leaned forward. "There he is."

"GOOD, WE FOUND him." He watched Milo concentrate at the screen loads that flashed faster than the human eye could see.

"No, we haven't."

"What? What do you mean? He's right there." Liev tapped the picture that had shown up. "That's his location."

"No. It's the location he's letting us see. He's not there now. In fact, I'd probably say he set that up as a decoy."

Liev groaned. "Not good." He turned away to glare around the kitchen. "What reason would he have for hiding like that? What is he afraid of? And why from me?"

Charming laughed. "The same reason you hide away. Because you are involved in something you want no one to know about."

Milo stared at Charming, considering his remarks. "In which case, Johan's likely the one behind all this. Maybe the one who actually supplies the pods." He turned to his brother. "Liev, what does Johan do?"

"Deals in trading. But I don't know what."

Lani made an odd sound. He turned to look at her, but she stared at Charming, who was already nodding. "Like Lawrence Blackburn. Part of the reason he was so oily was he used information like a weapon."

Liev stared at her. "What does Johan have to do with my ancestor?"

"Ah," Milo said. He turned back to the computer system. "That assumption is probably correct."

"What is correct?" Liev stared at the three of them. "What am I missing?"

Charming filled him in. "Johan and the pod that he freely lets his partygoers use and his disappearance all make sense if he is trading, ... buying, ... selling, ... information."

"Ah, hell."

CHAPTER 6

L ANI WONDERED WHAT kind of mess she'd fallen into. From Johan to Hahn to Gina. "I don't understand what Gina would gain by taking me to her office. If she is working with Johan what difference does it make? What purpose could they have?"

The two brothers shrugged. "I don't know either," Liev added. "Unless we weren't supposed to get there as fast as we did? Maybe someone else was arriving, and we beat them there," Liev said thoughtfully. "Milo?"

"Already on it."

Milo's fingers flashed so fast, Lani could hardly see what was happening. Her ever understanding Milo was a long way away.

"Ah, here it is again," Milo stated. "I'll let it stream longer. Should have thought to do that in the first place."

Before her was a recording of Gina's office. In silence, they watched as the video continued. Lani couldn't see a timestamp, but it hadn't been more than a couple minutes after the time she'd left with Liev when they heard another *pop*, and two men arrived.

She gasped. They looked dangerous. Unsavory.

Then again, it was a law office. They dealt with the criminal element all the time. Both men wore leather skin suits with heavy boots and chains hanging from their pockets. They were so typical-looking of the thugs from her day that she started to laugh.

Milo shushed her. "Let's listen."

The speaker replayed the conversation.

"Where is she?" asked the younger of the two men.

"How should I know?" said the older one. "The boss said she would be here."

She? Lani or Gina? And who was the boss?

While Lani tried to figure out what the men were talking about, Gina walked into view on-screen. She stared at the room and spun around in a full circle. In a shocked voice, she said, "Please tell me that you have her stashed somewhere."

Liev sucked in his breath. Lani looked up at him, watching as fury darkened his skin and tightened his features. But he never lifted his gaze from the screen. Lani returned her attention to the men talking.

"She wasn't here when we got here. Figured you had her in your private office." The man looked behind her. "Are you sure she didn't go in there with you?"

Gina glared at him, tiny beads of sweat forming on her brow.

If Lani hadn't been watching so closely, she doubt-ed she'd have seen them.

"Of course I'm sure." She spun around once more. "Damn it. Where could she be? No way those idiot brothers could have gotten to her first."

"Check the log. Then you'll know for sure."

She walked over to a wall, just off-screen. The two men turned to watch her, but they weren't close enough to read the log.

"Damn. It was them." Gina turned to face the men. "How could they have known she was here?"

Lani was confused. Gina knew Lani had left with Liev and Milo. *Why was she lying?*

"The obvious answer is, Lani told them," the first man said. "How else?"

"I scanned her when she arrived," Gina said. "She had no personal comp on her."

"Really? How bizarre is that?" Thug One asked. "Everyone has one."

"She must have left it behind at the Council," Thug Two said.

"What? So the brothers would find it and know that she's here somehow?" Gina asked sarcastically. "That makes no sense."

"Well, they knew somehow." Thug One looked bored.

"Tracker," Thug Two said. "She must have a tracker on her."

The three stared at each other.

"They wouldn't track just anyone," said Thug One in consideration. "She must be valuable."

"What she is, … is different," Gina said. "We need to know in what way."

The two men shrugged. "She can't be that different."

"Oh, she is. We just don't know how much or
why."

And the video stopped.

Silence ensued.

Then Milo exploded. "*Idiot* brothers?"

LIEV GRINNED. LANI laughed. Welcoming a chance to
lighten up after all the lies and deception. "Of course
that would be the one thing out of that entire conversation that you'd comment on," Lani quipped.

"I remember everything," he snapped. "I am *not* an
idiot."

Liev watched Lani and Milo spar. He listened with
only half an ear. His mind was consumed with what
he'd heard. How did anyone know about Lani? And
what did they know? Or thought they knew?

He'd been so careful. It had to be Johan, but what
good would that knowledge do for him? He had his
own troubles. Snatching Lani wouldn't help his case.

And why kidnap her? *Ransom?* Liev had money but
not billions. As far as he understood, Johan had more
money than Liev did. Johan knew about the tagging, so
that was probably where the leak had come from. Liev
had been afraid of problems from that corner but
hadn't expected it so quickly. Or from his neighbor.

Liev had done everything right. Lani should have been safe. She needed to be safe.

But apparently she wasn't even close.

Damn.

That Gina had been lying through her teeth was also worrisome. Was she trying to save her own skin so no one would know Lani had disappeared in her presence before the men arrived to take Lani away? Or was she playing a different, more dangerous game?

His mind spun. "Milo, we need to track Johan's movements, before and after he disappeared. Find out who he's been associating with, who he lives with now, who he lived with before. Details on his business pursuits. Even IDing partygoers at his house. Things like that. I hate to think he's behind all this, but we have to consider the possibility."

"For what purpose?" Lani asked him. "Would he have any concept of where I've come from really?" She lifted her shoulders slightly and dropped them. "Honestly, unless he knows the truth, and that's too bizarre for anyone to believe, what difference would my story make to him?"

"That's what we have to find out."

Milo tapped the screen, and a picture of Gina appeared. "She's the one who will know. We have to get this information to Hahn and corner her. If we show her the evidence we have on her, she'll break."

Liev saw a mature look come over his brother's features, a rare occurrence.

"I refuse to let this bitch do this to us."

"I don't know what penalties she'd face for this, but surely she'd turn on the others to save her own skin." Lani glanced at the photo. "Women like her are always more concerned about squeaking out of trouble themselves."

"True enough." Liev walked over to a blank wall and brought up his private HoloKomp system. "I'll get Hahn on the line. Milo, can you package up the section of video where the two men arrive in Gina's office? Cut it after she checked the log to see if we'd managed to get there before her henchmen. We'll show Hahn how she's been lying to both sides."

"Done," Milo said almost absently. "I've also isolated the henchmen's faces. Their tags have been shut down, so we can't identify them that way. I'll run a facial recognition program instead."

"Let's show their faces to Hahn as well," Lani said. "He might recognize them."

"Speaking of Hahn," Liev said to Milo, "make sure you initiate a body scan to see his vitals. He might be a good liar, but his body will show the effects of my questioning and seeing the men's faces."

Milo nodded. "No better lie detector in the world."

Lani gasped. "You can do all that?"

"And so much more. Watch and learn, sweetheart." Liev sent a link to Hahn. "He'll be online in a moment."

CHAPTER 7

LANI WATCHED AS Hahn's face appeared on the wall again. On the wall yet out of the wall in a very lifelike 3-D image.

"What now?" Hahn snapped. "I'm still trying to get ahold of Gina."

"This." And Liev set the video screen to Play. "It's just after Milo and I left Gina's office."

In front of Lani, projected on a wall for Hahn to see, the two thugs appeared in Gina's office almost magically. Another holographic projection but large enough for Hahn to see. Lani really wanted to learn to use those ports. She would love to travel if it was instantaneous. She'd had some initial stomach reactions, but presumably that would get better over time. At least she hoped her physical reactions would calm down.

She studied Hahn's face, wondering at the clarity of the image that made it seem like he was right inside the room. It was on the tip of her tongue to ask. Maybe they even had interplanetary travel. Now that would be so cool. Honestly, what she'd seen outside had scared her, but, at the same time, it was exciting.

As long as she was safely inside. Though, by this time, she realized that she'd only seen a tiny portion of what the technology of today's world could do.

As the video played out in front of him, Hahn gasped in shock, his skin turning a pasty gray. Once he spoke, he didn't waste any unnecessary words. "That's Paul and Tommy Defino. They're on the run after escaping prison transport. Both are wanted for breaking and entering, armed robbery, and a host of other charges."

"Did you represent them? Did Gina? Is there any other viable reason why they'd be in your offices and communicating in this manner with your business associate?" At Liev's cutting tone, Lani turned slightly so she could see his face.

This angry Liev took some getting used to. He stood tall and arrogant, his arms crossed over his chest as he challenged Hahn. Irate but in control. Someone had messed up, and he'd know the reason why.

He handled power well. It emanated from him in long-reaching waves. He knew what he could do and how to get what he wanted in life. Something was very attractive about that.

She understood he ran the large company he and his brother founded, and that had to have molded him. For the first time, she could see the businessman who'd carved a place for himself in the corporate world.

Hahn shook his head. "No. I won't have that element in my company. I've been trying to locate Gina, but, so far, she's not answering her personal comp, her home comp, or her car's communication system. I don't know where she's gone."

Liev shot Milo a look. He grinned and shambled over to the large countertop, flexed his fingers, and got to work. Lani was torn between watching Liev verbally bat Hahn around and racing to Milo's side to watch him perform magic. She'd always had a love for technology but hadn't realized her interest was this strong. And the stuff she now saw ...

Her fascination won out, and she raced to Milo's side. He moved screen loads and clicked parts of the countertop where she couldn't see that it had any buttons. She presumed he was busy tracking down the bitchy lawyer on one set of monitors and running scans on Hahn at the same time. She could see a heat scanner but it was holding steady with only slight variations in temperature. It had stabilized on the red edge. Hahn was pissed.

Lani didn't want to cause anyone else trouble. *Live and let live* was her motto. But, if they weren't going to leave her alone, then all bets were off.

Still, she wished she understood what Milo was doing.

He pounded on the countertop, making her back up, afraid the monitor thingy would break. Instead, the huge flat display opened up like a 3-D box, rising straight up from the counter. She gasped in delight and wonder. Milo went into action, sweeping screen loads to the side and bringing up more. His hands danced in and out of the blue-green images that flowed from the box. She noted that Milo had some facial recognition software down on one side. He was looking for the missing lawyer just in a different way than his search for Johan. And Lani wanted him to find her.

She bent over and studied the pictures as they whipped by. Now he flicked the pictures like a movie stream, and the computer tossed in ones of the males from the search for the Defino brothers she'd seen in the video. Her mind saw it before her eyes recognized it.

She reached out and stabbed a picture before it disappeared off the side of the counter. "That one."

"What one?" Milo dragged it toward him and blew up the image. It was the profile of one of the men. Oddly enough, it had been the snake's head earring she'd recognized.

A long, low whistle slipped from Milo's lips. "Nice. That's the older one, Paul. Now to source his location."

Once again screen loads went flying. Just when a headache settled in for good into Lani's brain from trying to watch all the flying images, Liev turned off the video screen with Hahn and joined them.

He stood on the other side of Milo. "No sign of her?"

"Not yet. We've found him though." Milo reached up and tapped the image in the corner. As he did, Charming jumped up on the countertop. "Whoa,"

Milo said. "No cats on the monitor."

Charming backed up slightly to the edge but did not jump off. He stared at the images, his whiskers vibrating.

She didn't know if he planned on jumping on the flashing images or if he understood what they were looking for and could help. She didn't want to ask, but her attention was caught on Charming as he stared at the fast-paced screens in front of him. Then his paw flashed out, and he dragged an image back toward him.

"Hey, no scratching the monitor," Milo cried out.

"I didn't scratch it." Charming sniffed. "Besides, I can't. It's holographic." He released the image. "I believe this is who you are looking for." He sat back and proceeded to clean the paw he'd touched the monitor with.

Everyone leaned over the picture. The image was too small for her to see. Liev reached over and tapped it twice. The image blew up.

Gina.

Milo stared at Charming. "Wow. Like seriously good."

Liev snorted. "And who made him like that?"

Milo snickered. "Good point. We're all good."

"Yeah, right," Lani said.

"Hey, you found this guy. I didn't." Milo beamed at her, as if she were a prized student.

"Really?" Liev looked at her with added respect. "That's great. Trying to find images when Milo gets going is not easy."

She grinned. How could she not? At least she wasn't a complete loser.

Charming shot her a direct look. She flushed. Surely he couldn't read minds now, could he? He went back to his grooming. As she looked around the kitchen, what she really wanted was some of that awesome coffee. She'd come out looking for some earlier, but, with everything going on, she'd gotten distracted.

She walked around behind the men. At the other side, she studied the flat wall, looking for anything to denote cupboards, coffeemakers, or even a water spout.

And found nothing.

"LANI, WHAT DO you need?" Liev asked, circling the counter to stand beside her. He wanted to take her in his arms and kiss her, but something stopped him. Maybe it was the fact that she'd so done well with Milo.

Not everyone did. Maybe it was Charming, who'd shifted his position so he could stare right at Liev. Stupid to be nervous of a cat. But there it was.

Even odder that the cat had managed to snag Gina's picture out of the thousands floating past. Liev would have to talk to Milo about what exact enhancement he had given the cat.

"I was looking for a drink."

"Water?" He walked to the wall. "Watch." She

stepped closer to see a break in the paint. It was a scrolled-style circle. He pressed his hand flat on the wall and pressed down. Instantly, a cupboard popped out. He removed a tall skinny glass and moved over several feet. While she watched, he pushed another section of wall, and a small fountain slid out with a hand attachment. He squeezed the attachment, and her glass filled with water. "See? It's easy. Every space in today's world is designed to multitask."

"Like anything new, it is easy if you know how. Is this filtered?" she asked.

"Absolutely." Like everything in their world, water was severely regulated, being one of the last few natural resources left to them. They had to protect it. But she didn't need to know that right now. She'd quickly be overloaded with information.

She tossed back the drink and held the glass out again. He refilled it and handed it over. She sipped the second glass. "Is there any chance of getting coffee?"

His face lit up. "Oh, good idea. That's exactly what we need." He turned around to make the first of what he expected would be several pots. He'd have to look into buying a bigger unit.

Yet none of the changes he would be making were anything like the ones Lani had gone through, so he couldn't complain.

He ordered coffee with a push of a button. Lani was quiet behind him. He wondered at her conspicuous silence over their marriage deal. Then he'd avoided the topic altogether. Once he'd gotten her agreement and had pushed through the process he'd left the subject alone. It was a land mine waiting to explode and needed delicate handling. He'd almost brought it up in the pod room earlier, but it hadn't been the most pressing issue then, so he'd held back. Maybe she was hoping it would go away.

Whereas he was hoping to resume the honeymoon. He couldn't help but think about the many benefits of being married. And how hot and willing she'd been in his arms. God, he wanted that again. And soon. Like now. He slid a gaze her way. She'd settled back to watch him, as he made coffee her gaze intent on his motions. And, damn, if that intensity wasn't a turn-on.

Just then, her stomach grumbled. At first he didn't recognize the sound. Then it sank in. He froze. Uh-oh. Lani had been pulled from bed, taken to the Council, kidnapped, and returned home to recuperate in the pod—all on an empty stomach. Checking the comp on his wrist, he winced and said, "You missed another meal, didn't you?"

"Two meals," Charming whined from the monitor counter.

Liev nodded. True enough. "Right. Coffee first. Then food."

Charming howled at the sound of food being placed second. "How can you put coffee first?" he moaned. "I need *foooood.*"

CHAPTER 8

L ANI CHUCKLED AT Charming, walking closer to him to scratch his neck. "You hadn't even noticed that you were missing a meal until it was mentioned."

"Of course I noticed," Charming said, turning his neck for her to get at another spot.

How did a cat manage to look affronted? Lani shook her head and scooped him up. She stared down into those eyes, so familiar and yet so different now. She recognized her wonderful old tomcat in there, but, at the same time, someone different was there. Someone even better. Her heart swelled as she held him close. "I'm so glad you survived that trip."

"Me too," he whispered, rubbing against her neck. "Like what would have happened to me if you came here, and I was left locked in the apartment?"

A shudder swept through her. "That would have been horrible. You'd have died without me to take care of you."

"And yet today, I took care of you." He reared back and pinned her with a beady eye. "So I should get your share of lunch."

She laughed. "So not happening." She carried him

over toward Liev, who appeared to be making sand-wiches. At the sight of the thick slabs of bread and cheese, Charming moaned louder.

"With all the technology you have available, how is it you are doing the cooking?" Lani asked.

"It's a hobby." He flushed, then shrugged uncom-fortably. "It's a bit of a joke to my friends actually."

"So there is an alternative."

That made him laugh. "Yes. We have machines that create complete meals now. I just don't want to have one around."

"Oh." She personally would love a machine that could do it all. Then again, if he was happy to cook, she was happy to let him.

"He's into retro stuff. Like food and cooking," Milo spoke up. "It takes work, and it's disgusting."

Lani laughed. She looked at Liev and shared a look of understanding. "Unless it's chocolate, I suppose."

Milo scowled. "Chocolate is different."

"The food is almost ready. Give me another mi-nute." Liev reached for a large block of something. She leaned in, then realized what it was. "Oh, yum. Roast beef."

He gave her a strange look. "Did they have that in your time?"

She stared at him. "Of course." Then she frowned. "This is from an animal, isn't it?"

He looked at the block of meat and then back at her.

And she realized it was square in shape. As in, very square. As in, too square. "Oh, damn. This isn't meat, is it?"

"Meat is bad for you," Milo said from the other side of the counter. "I've told you that. Boosters are better—in all ways."

"Except that Charming is a carnivore," Lani reminded him. "And so am I."

"He could drink boosters too." Milo appeared to be warming up to one of his favorite subjects.

Charming said in a low voice, "Let's go back to the meat."

"Except I'm not sure it's meat."

"Oh, it's meat," Liev said, "and it came from an animal but not a live one."

Dumbfounded, Lani could only stare at the block of gray stuff. "Like cloned meat?"

"Ha! More likely 3-D printed meat," Charming said with a snicker. He sniffed the air experimentally, caught a whiff, and started to wiggle out of her arms. "Except that would be old tech here. And this smells delicious."

"Hey, wait. You're going to fall." She tightened her grip.

"Let me go, and I'll jump."

He tried to sneak out of her arms, but she clamped down tight and said, "No animals where the food is. We'll sit at the table. He'll bring food when it's ready." She walked him back to the table where they'd eaten their first meal.

"I could be dead by then," Charming groaned.

"And they might happily kill you if you don't behave yourself," she snapped. "Remember your manners."

"And maybe they should remember theirs," he retorted. "Considering that we are the guests, and they are the hosts." He peered around Lani's body to stare at Liev's back. "Lousy hosts at that."

She gasped in horror. "You apologize right now. That is not acceptable. You know perfectly well that he's preparing our meal. Now be appreciative of that fact before you lose out completely, based on your bad behavior."

"*Harrumph.*" Charming stared up at her. "I'm not a two-year-old. You can't treat me like that."

Milo laughed from behind her.

She tilted her head toward the sound. "Do you hear that? That's because, although you're not that age, it's how old you are acting."

Charming's marble eyeballs hid behind his suddenly slitted eyelids. He howled deep in the back of his throat.

"Stop it. Communication is new for you. I get it." She dropped a kiss on top of his head. "That's okay. You'll get the hang of it, and, besides, you'll always be my adorable kitty."

"Oh, brother." He turned away from her to pad over to the farthest point on the kitchen table. "This could get embarrassing if you're getting all mushy."

Her laughter pealed out to ring around the room. Without warning, she reached across and scooped him back into her arms. She started to dance, like they did in their previous life, holding Charming in her arms, as if he were a human-size partner with one paw up. "It so could get mushy. Because I love you. I always have. You are my best friend. And, now that you can talk, I so want us to have a tea party and to play dress up …"

At his shocked shriek, she bent over, giggling, still holding him in her arms. He dug his claws in, probably as a punishment. She straightened, the odd giggle still pouring out. "You are too funny. I was only kidding, by the way."

"You'd better be," he threatened, curling his claws ever-so-slightly.

"Watch the nails," she said in warning.

"Why? You have a healing pod now. I can cause all kinds of damage, and you'll be just fine." He stretched up to stare into her eyes.

Would she ever get used to him being able to talk like this? She hoped so, but she also didn't want to lose the pet she'd had since forever. Emotion washed over her, and she wrapped him up tight. Against his fur, she whispered, "I'm so glad you're mine."

His engine kicked in and made the tears once again burn her eyes.

When he whispered, "Me too," that made her heart melt.

LIEV STOPPED TO watch the two interact. He couldn't believe the language coming out of Charming's mouth. Damn, he needed to corner Milo and ask him about those enhancements. He remembered Milo's slip of the tongue earlier. If he knew his brother, Milo wouldn't stop at one enhancement if he had a chance to slide more in. Considering how quickly Charming had locked on that image on the screen, Liev had to wonder if eagle vision or super-quick reflexes might have been one of the other enhancements. And that would suck for Lani if the cat had received all the benefits. Imagine knowing that your cat was smarter, faster, and more intelligent than you were.

Talk about a major turn in their relationship.

Yet he remembered Lani had snagged a picture from Milo's fast-moving stream as well, so maybe they'd both received enhancements. They could have shown up stronger on Charming, due to his size in relation to Lani's.

Liev watched the two cuddle, and, for the first time in his life, he saw something lacking in his. He'd never had a pet. He'd had a stuffed teddy bear for his first couple years, until he'd been deemed old enough to go without. And now, as he watched Lani cuddle Charming, he realized how much the cat enriched Lani's life. And quite possibly that worked both ways.

Just then, Charming's head popped up over Lani's shoulder, and that golden gaze locked on his.

Even before the cat opened his mouth, Liev knew

what would come out. He held up heaping plates of food and walked closer. Charming's eyes rounded in delight, and he scrambled to get out of Lani's arms and onto the table.

"He's got food," Charming said urgently, when Lani resisted.

She laughed and set him on the table. "Let's eat then." As she took her place at the table, she asked, "Liev, can I help you do anything?"

"It's done. Not to worry. You can help next time. These are just simple sandwiches."

Milo walked past. "And I'll make boosters for both of you while I get mine."

Liev happened to be watching both Lani and Charming, so he saw them wrinkle their faces in disgust. Catching his eye though, they both grinned. Lani said, "We'll drink it because we need it, but honestly, food is more our style."

She motioned to Charming, who busily gnawed on thick chunks of ham that Liev had found for him to accompany his serving of beef as well.

"I need to get cat food for him," Liev said.

Charming lifted his head and stared at him in horror. "I eat protein. Not cat food. *Protein.* Chicken. Fish. Lamb. Mice." He stared more intently, just to make sure Liev understood the seriousness of the issue. "Understand?"

Liev raised one eyebrow and nodded. "Got it."

Chapter 9

L ANI HAD FINALLY filled up enough to know that she would make it another day. She wasn't so sure about Charming, as he'd finished his second helping and right now plowed through a third. For herself, the fatigue had returned in triplicate. The pod seemed too far away to reach, and her eyelids already drooped.

Before she had a chance to decide if sleeping where she sat for a few moments was a good idea or not, she was scooped up and carried into the tiny healing room. She snuggled against Liev's chest. "Sorry. Just got so tired all of a sudden."

"Hey, it was a tough morning for us all." He shifted her in his arms. "An afternoon nap is perfect."

She heard a series of buttons clicking, then a low hum. The healing pod. She so wanted to be in there. And, just like that, he laid her inside and dropped a kiss on her forehead. She smiled sleepily, closed her eyes, and let her mind drift off.

She heard the door shut behind Liev as he exited. In the distance were sounds of conversation, but it was far enough out of her hearing that she couldn't make out the words.

Drifting was nice, easy. She heard a weird sound, then felt something small hit her arm. She rubbed her arm, then rolled over to get more comfortable, loving the way the bed adjusted beneath her. What a marvelous invention. Several small noises outside the pod bothered her, but a buffer created by the pod's humming noise filtered those out. It was great.

But maybe not *quite* great. Her eyes opened. Something didn't feel right.

She didn't feel right.

But she didn't know what was wrong.

"Charming? Are you here?" He'd said he'd follow her in a few minutes, when Liev had carried her in this direction—but had he?

It felt like … someone was here.

As that knowledge filtered in, she realized that someone definitely was, but it was not someone she knew. Or rather, wasn't someone who was supposed to be in here.

Shit.

Her breath caught in the back of her throat. What was she supposed to do? She could slip out of the pod and make a run for the door, but it wasn't like that would be a subtle move. They'd see her. And maybe that was okay. Just because a stranger was in here didn't mean they were out to get her. Except everyone who had been a stranger so far had been out to do just that.

She could lie here and pretend to be asleep.

Gently she rubbed the sore spot on her arm.

She felt exposed. What if this person grabbed her by her feet? That thought whirled inside her head, making her almost blind with fear. Slowly she pulled her feet up toward her chest. Her breathing became raspy. The more she tried to control her breathing, the worse it got. The pod lights changed from blue to purple, and immediately more heat beat down on top of her. The pod knew she was under stress. Her vitals had to be off the chart again. At the same time, she knew that had to be a signal to whoever was in here with her. She saw no sign of Charming still.

Would he recognize that her vital signs had gone crazy again? Or was he still eating like he wouldn't get another meal? She closed her eyes and starting calling him in her mind. *Charming, please help. Charming, can you hear me? Please, someone, come.*

She took another long shuddery breath, surprised to find she'd curled up into a fetal position. She would feel like a fool if everyone came racing into the room, and she was actually alone.

But she'd rather that than the opposite. She wondered how she could bolt out the door without getting caught.

Then a noise sounded behind the pod. *Oh, God. Oh, God. Oh, God!*

She froze. And couldn't catch her breath. She had never had a panic attack, but this was starting to be a full-on scream-for-her-life-and-run moment.

As quietly and as naturally as she could, she slid

over to the edge of the pod bed.

Stiff, barely breathing, she readied her muscles and slowly pushed the pod lid open just a little bit.

Three, two, one …

She slid under the edge of the pod and bolted for the open door, screaming at the top of her lungs.

"WHAT IS THAT?" Charming sat up abruptly from his cleaning to stare in the direction of the pod room. Liev and Milo raced down the short hallway, where Lani ran smack into Liev's chest. He caught her in his arms, while trying to see what had scared her. "Milo, check out the room."

"No, no, he shouldn't go alone," Lani cried out. "Someone's in there."

"What? Impossible." Liev shook his head as he held her close. "No one else is here. It's not possible."

She shuddered in his arms. "It's not only possible, it's real. I could hear their breathing and weird noises." She slapped her hand over her arm. "I swear something hit my arm."

"What?" Liev stepped back and lifted her arm so he could see. "There's no way."

But there was. A slight red spot showed on her upper arm. He tucked her close to him and moved her into the kitchen. "Stay here." He walked to a wall and brought up his security system with a few commands.

"Milo, where are you?" he asked.

The intercom broadcasted his voice. Liev set the computer to show all the occupants in his house. Immediately the gray screen lit up several orange hot spots. He easily identified himself and Lani. Charming had to be the smaller one.

And there was Milo in the pod room.

"I'm right here, Liev," Milo said as he walked into the kitchen. "Nothing's there."

Liev shut down the intercom, sealed off the pod room, and motioned his brother to come over to him. He tapped the monitor at the red image in the pod room and, in a low voice, asked, "Then what or who is this?"

CHAPTER 10

L ANI HUDDLED AT the kitchen table. Charming sat in front of her, but his attention was on the brothers behind her, checking out the apartment still via their computer security network. She'd rather be back in Liev's arms. A chill rippled up and down her arms. She rubbed them, wishing she understood what the guys were talking about. Had she just imagined an intruder? The pod room was barely big enough for anyone else to stand in, let alone hide.

And why hadn't she seen someone if they were there?

None of it made any sense. The fact remained; her arm stung from whatever had happened to it. Liev walked over, ran a gentle finger over her arm, and frowned. He asked, "The healing pod didn't fix this?"

"Not sure it had time," she admitted. "And I'm not going back in there until I know it's safe."

"We need to know what caused it."

"And how do we do that?" She stared down at the puffy skin on her arm. It was a tiny injury. Not worth making a fuss about. Still ... "Whatever this was, my body doesn't like it."

"I'll take another look with Milo."

Charming jumped up on the table beside her and rubbed his head against her shoulder. "Hey, Charming. Wish you'd been in there with me?"

"I hate strangers. You know that."

"True, you used to always run away." She rubbed her cheek against his head. "Except you like Liev and Milo just fine."

His engine kicked in when she kissed the top of his head.

"They are different," he said with a yawn, dropping his butt on the table and looking around with interest. "Do you think they have any leftovers?"

"Probably, but keep eating like a crazy man, and they will be forced to keep canned cat food around for you."

He looked at her through slitted eyes. "You mean, canned shrimp and tuna, right?"

She shook her head. "I don't know why they would. Besides, you loved canned cat food before."

"Sure, but they don't have that food here. And," he leaned in, tilting his head so he could whisper in her ear, "what if Milo picks the food? It's likely to be green and full of boosters."

At that, she giggled. And, boy, did that feel good. From fear to laughter in a heartbeat. She caught a glimpse of the satisfaction in Charming's gaze. "You did that on purpose." she accused.

"Did not." He twisted and started grooming his

back.

"Did too," she muttered.

"So what? Someone has to do something to keep your mind off the intruder."

Intruder? It sounded way worse when he said it. More real.

"Nope. It wasn't." Charming continued to clean, sounding completely unconcerned.

So you can *read my mind?* she asked, watching him.

He gave her one of those *Duh* looks.

She sighed. Charming had at least three enhancements that she had discovered so far. "Then who was it?" she asked in an ominous tone of voice.

"Not sure," Charming said, "but I think it was a what, not a who."

Puzzled, she stared at him, wishing he'd pay attention and stop cleaning his butt. "How could that have been anything but a person?"

"Holograph," Charming said.

Wordlessly, she stared at her four-year-old cat, who appeared to understand things way beyond her comprehension.

Into the sudden silence, he paused what he was doing and lifted his head to pin her gaze with his. "What?"

"How would you know that?"

Damn if his nose didn't go up in the air before he returned to his cleaning.

Apparently she didn't warrant an answer.

LIEV STRODE DOWN the hallway, Milo close on his heels. At the pod room doorway, he stopped and gently pushed open the door as wide as it would go. He couldn't see anything, but the computer scan wouldn't have made a mistake like this.

"I don't see anything," Milo said. He almost pushed Liev into the room as he craned to see over his shoulder. "There has to be a glitch."

"I wouldn't be so sure about that." Liev stepped into the room and bent to look below the pod. He couldn't see anything with the naked eye. But ... he clicked through the screen loads on his wrist comp and found the same disturbing hot spot. Above and behind the pod.

He walked around until he was directly under the spot. He twisted his head, trying to see into the dark corner, when a light shone right on him. Startled, he turned to see Milo lighting the spot in question. Liev pivoted when something beeped behind him. "What the ...?"

"It's my new toy." Milo held up the base of the light to show him the flashing buttons that accompanied the beeps. "It's a bug finder."

Liev stared at his brother before switching his gaze from the device to the high corner of the ceiling. "Bugs?" he asked in a hard voice. "Here? After all the sweeps and security measures we have in place?"

Milo leaned closer and whispered in his ear, "Probably came in with the pod."

Damn. As he thought about it, it made perfect sense. He'd been so worried about taking this step and hoping it was the answer to help Lani that he'd not run through any of the special security checks. The normal ones, sure. But who had time to consider beyond that? He hadn't had a chance to think about anything, ... let alone act on the thoughts.

He stared, wondering what to do next. Milo motioned him to retreat the same way he did. Back out in the hallway, Milo closed the door and pressed several buttons on his little gadget. Liev had built-in bug sweepers that he used often. His office and home were wired to catch any that made their way inside, but this one ...

He smiled reassuringly at Lani, Charming in her arms, standing hesitantly at the end of the hallway. They'd obviously followed him and Milo to see what they'd found.

"It's very high tech," Milo muttered as he popped open a 3-D screen. Then he stepped back to walk around the image. "These are the blueprints of the bug."

Liev stared. "It was inside the unit. Meant to break off as the bug was released from its hiding spot." He turned to face Lani. "The casing is what hit her arm."

"It has audio." Charming sauntered closer, making Liev back away. "So it can hear us. ... Meaning, we should be able to hear it."

Milo spun around and stared at the damn cat in excitement. "That's right. I can track it back, using its own programming code."

And damn if that cat didn't sit back on its haunches and nod his head approvingly at Milo. Liev felt like the dummy in the class—again. Milo hadn't been the easiest brother to live with. "Can you find out who sent this?"

"Not only that, I might be able to listen in on what's going on in their office or wherever they are holding the receiver for this unit."

"I didn't see a bug in there." Liev hated to bring it up, but … "How small could it be?"

"It's holographic and invisible."

Liev, in the act of walking back to the kitchen, froze. "What did you say?"

"It's an invisible holographic bug," Milo said impatiently.

"And that doesn't sound incredibly wrong to you?"

Milo shook his head slowly, as if to clear his head so he could focus. "We have invisibility, and we have bugs and holographs. Someone put them all together."

"And that someone wasn't you?" Maybe that was the biggest surprise here. Liev had never known anyone to get the edge on Milo in a field he loved, and espionage toys were one of his specialties.

"Nah, no point in adding holograph stuff. Just a waste of time."

That almost made more sense. It wasn't a practical application. With a smile, Liev continued down the hallway, gently moving a very confused Lani ahead of him, until he realized what his brother didn't say. He spun around and continued to walk backward. "Wait? What about the invisible part?"

"What about it?" Milo was busy with his little toy.

"Have you managed to make an invisible bug?" Liev tried to hang on to his patience, but his brother could try a saint. "Like this one?"

"Not like this one."

Liev waited.

"Better." And Milo shot him a quirky grin of success. He didn't punch the air with his fist, but it was damn close.

"Better how?" He couldn't see how an invisible bug could be improved on. He waited, but Milo busily chuckled and clicked away on his fingerboard comp, matching it to something happening on his bug finder. Liev waited a moment, then nudged his brother. "Milo, how could you make a better bug than an invisible one?"

Milo looked up in surprise. "I just expanded on your idea."

As he looked to be returning to the toys in his hand, Liev quickly interjected, "What are you talking about?"

"Stealth technology. *Duh*. On a microscale."

And he walked back into the pod room, leaving Liev to stare after him in shock. He'd developed the home stealth technology system to cloak what they were doing in the company and at home. It was a military-type application, but he'd refined it for their purposes, and apparently Milo had refined it yet again. He trailed behind his brother. "So you can send in an invisible bug *and* have it receive and send data without anyone picking up its presence with any tracking device?"

Milo stopped and threw his head back in frustration. "That's what I just said, didn't I?"

Liev snorted. "Not really."

"Well, it's what I meant. Now, if you don't mind, I'd like to listen in on our uninvited visitor." Shooting Liev a dark look, Milo walked forward until he stood just below the spot. Adjusting the monitor, strange voices filled the room.

"I can't tell what's happening. There's been only static for the last bit."

"Any chance they found the bug?"

A snort came first. "Hell no. This baby isn't even on the market."

Liev cocked his head, trying to figure out who was speaking. He brought up his own comp and set up to record the next bit of conversation.

"Maybe it's broken."

"And maybe you should pull your brain out of your butt and use it once in a while."

"Watch your mouth. You might think you are the best of the best, but someone better is always out there. You can be replaced."

That sharp retort was followed by footsteps and a door slamming.

"Ass."

Liev checked his comp to find he had enough to run a voice recognition program. He started it and looked over to see what Milo was up to. He'd held up his bug finder as high as he could to the ceiling.

A weird ear-splitting sound filled the room.

And then came dead silence.

Chapter 11

L ANI DIDN'T UNDERSTAND what was going on. A virtual invader? Like, how was that possible? It was hard to be scared of someone jumping out and attacking you if just an image. She'd followed the two brothers as they'd wrangled their way down the hallway. She had heard their discussion and then some other voices. It didn't make complete sense, but it appeared that something extra had come in with the pod. And that wasn't likely to be good.

Then the room filled with a horrific noise. She clapped her hands over her ears and crouched on her heels. Just as suddenly, the noise stopped, and the silence was almost as painful. She shuddered when something touched her. She turned to see Charming rubbing up against her leg. "That didn't bother you?"

"No, not the same way it did you."

"And I thought animals had better hearing."

"Sure we do, but I also knew it was coming, so I had time to prepare for it."

"You knew it ahead of time?" She shook her head at her cat. "How is that possible?"

And damn if he didn't give her that look that said

she was too stupid to bother explaining it to. She shot a glare at his back and stood up as the brothers came out. "What was that?"

Liev wrapped an arm around her shoulder, turning her toward the kitchen. "Milo just killed a bug."

She twisted so she could see his face. "You mean, an espionage-type thing?" At his nod, she raised her eyebrows. "Are you two so heavy into this stuff that people are trying to steal information about Milo's inventions, or is this about me?"

"I don't know. Both are possible. I just don't know how they knew the pod was coming here to have something like that ready in time."

Charming galloped down the hallway in front of them. "What's to understand? The bug and pod came from the same person. If you needed an unregistered pod, they needed a bug in here to find out why!"

"That's getting old," Lani muttered, glaring at her beloved know-it-all pet.

His tail flicked in several sharp motions as if to say, *Get over it.*

"He's right though." Milo sauntered past. "It had to have been ready to go before you ordered the pod—or right at the same time. I told you it was a bad idea."

Liev pulled up short. Lani turned, about to ask him what was wrong when he said, "This is getting damn old."

She grinned. "Milo might have brought me for you, but it looks like he brought Charming for himself."

Liev's gaze widened, and he broke out laughing. "That is so true."

They entered the kitchen to find identical looks on Milo's and Charming's faces. As if reading each other's minds in tandem, they turned their backs on Lani and Liev.

She giggled freely, loving it when Liev hugged her close. "Let's go see if the two geniuses can figure this out."

Still smirking, they stepped up to the side of the big holographic monitor that the two smarties studied.

"My voice recognition hasn't found anything yet," Liev volunteered.

"And it won't most likely. You don't have the latest software."

"What?" Liev stared at his comp. "Sure I do. This was just updated last month."

"And I updated it after trying to find Gina's henchmen buddies." Milo lifted his head to Liev's glare. "What? I sent it to you. It's not my fault if you didn't do the upgrade as you were supposed to."

"There aren't supposed to be any. It's supposed to be seamless. Remember?"

Liev's deceptively soft tone had Lani searching his face, not understanding the undercurrents. "Updating computer software was constant in my world. Is that the same here?" she asked.

"No," Liev said, his voice more resigned than hard. "It's part of Milo's mockery of my retro preferences."

"Not totally. It's fun to bug you, but it is safer right now to do things manually. You know that. If we have a problem, we have to go into blackout mode. And that means taking everything off-line and updating manually."

"Damn."

Milo laughed. "See? You forgot."

"Well, I've had other things to worry about."

Milo reached out, flicked a couple of holo buttons, and pulled a holo headset out of the monitor and wrapped it around the back of his head. He brought up some white screen and, with his hands not touching the monitor or the keyboard, words started to appear.

"What the heck?" she muttered, leaning closer. "What's he doing?"

"Recording his observations and planning what to do next."

Lani shook her head. "But his fingers aren't moving."

Liev stared at her. "What does his fingers have to do with it?"

"Ah, … typing?" She gave him a look that should have made him understand the problem, but instead he grinned. "At least audio for speech."

He laughed. "Sorry, typing is old-school."

"Just like me, apparently." She watched as paragraphs of text appeared on one side of this big monitor. "So you can just think what you want onto that screen?"

"Sure. Works much better."

"I can see that." She stared, trying to figure out how it worked. "It must be set up for his neural impulses."

"Exactly." Charming looked at her in admiration. "I didn't think you could figure that out."

"Watch it," she warned. Then had to smile as his face split into a huge feline grin. "You were teasing me, weren't you?"

He nodded before turning around on the spot and lying down. Just before he closed his eyes, he whispered, "Nap time."

"I wish."

Liev reached an arm across her shoulders. "You can go back in the pod."

Wistfully, she considered the idea. "Is it safe?"

"Absolutely. Come on. I'll take you back."

She let him lead her back into the small room. "It doesn't feel the same."

"No, but it is fine. It's safe and secure. The sounds you heard were coming from the bug."

"But it sounded like heavy breathing."

"Probably just the initial sounds as it went live. The bug had no visual on it, so it couldn't see into the room. But it did have audio."

At her shocked look, he rushed to reassure her. "They didn't hear much. It just turned on now while you were in there."

"It could have been on then too." She leaned in and whispered, "You know? When …"

"No." He shook his head. "The bug would have showed up earlier on our house comp, if that were the case. I had to run all sorts of security programs with the raid and the warrant. No. It was turned on just a few minutes ago."

"Are you sure?" Because she wasn't. "What a horrible thought to think someone was listening in like that."

"They weren't," he reassured her. "It was installed in the pod, to detach at the right time."

Inside the room, he opened the pod. "I have something special to make you feel better."

She slid him a sideways look, wondering what he meant by that. But he appeared to be studying the computer dashboard on the pod. "Go ahead and lie down," he said, his fingers dancing on the keyboard.

Desperate to have the soothing sensation the pod could provide, she scrambled inside and immediately felt better. She had to trust that the Blackburn brothers knew what they were doing.

Then again, she didn't have much choice.

LIEV WAITED UNTIL Lani had stretched out in the pod. He needed her to relax enough to be back in here. Afraid or not, she still needed the pod and likely would for a long time to come.

He played a gentle music track and set the pod to

give a massage.

She moaned. "I don't know what you did, but it feels wonderful."

"It will massage whatever surface you lay on the pod. So a back massage or a chest massage."

"Then I'm good here for a long time."

He smiled. "It will help you to sleep too." He backed away toward the door when she asked, "You're sure it's safe?"

"I'm sure. Just rest."

He waited a few moments, studying the small room and realizing how unimpressive it was. He could fix that. He could also make the room bigger. His head reeling with ideas, he snuck out of the room and headed directly to the big computer.

There, working on the opposite side of Milo, he brought up the dimensions of the apartment. He had paid extra for the adjustable space, and, so far, they hadn't used it all. He enlarged the space of the pod room, incorporating the bed she'd slept in the first night to make a bedroom big enough for Lani and the pod. As much as he'd love to have her in his bedroom—she was his wife, after all—he wanted that to be her decision. So until that time, ... he opened the decorating program, studied the settings, and selected a Pacific island hideaway. He started the program, hoping she was asleep already. Otherwise the changes might freak her out. He should have thought of it earlier.

As it was, he realized he'd better check up on her.

He quickly raced down to the room and watched as the colors changed and as the holograph appearance shifted so the pod was in the middle of a South Pacific island. The walls also slowly adapted to the new parameters he'd set, allowing the imagery to have more punch. He thought the sand was a nice touch. He noticed that Charming had followed him into the pod room.

"*Ohh*, a litter box." Charming jumped in.

"No! That's not a litter box," Liev whispered in a harsh tone.

"Looks like a litter box." Charming walked forward and sniffed. "Smells like a litter box." He turned in a circle and started to dig. "Feels like a litter box." And he squatted.

"No! Don't do that." Liev hurriedly opened his link to the comp programming back in the kitchen. "Program. No sand. No sand!"

Too late.

Charming flicked his butt, lifted his nose in the air, and sighed happily. "Nice litter box." He studiously buried his mess, then bolted past Liev.

Liev groaned. "I can't believe you did that," he yelled after Charming. "You know better."

"Who knows what better?" Lani stuck just her head out from under the pod, frowning at him. "I was asleep. What happe—" She stopped. Her eyes went wide, and she gasped. "Oh my. What happened in here?"

"It was supposed to be a surprise."

"It's a fantastic surprise," she exclaimed. "But why?

How?" She pulled herself farther out to stare in happy amazement. "We're not really in the South Pacific, are we? If we are, I'm all for staying here."

He smiled at her innocence. "No, we aren't. But, if you want to go, just say the word."

"*Word*," she cried out happily, bouncing on the bed inside the pod. "Word. Word. Word."

He stepped over Charming's heaped sand pile and opened the pod. "Sorry. I didn't mean today. Later we'll travel. A lot of things need to be taken care of here first."

She stared up at him, lying back on the pod bed. "Really? It's not expensive?"

His eyebrows shot up. She really had no idea what kind of wealth he and his brother had accumulated, or that she herself had, for that matter. "Let's just say it's definitely doable." He thought about the benefit of taking her where no one else would know who they were, until she learned more about their world. "And it might not be a bad idea. I'll have to think about the ramifications."

"No, you have to work. I understand. You can't just take time off whenever you feel like it."

She really didn't understand. He needed to fill in her education and fast. "There's a lot you need to learn about the family business, but, for the moment, I can work anywhere in the world. I can show up to work in holographic form. That's how I attend most meetings. Yes, we have offices, as you know, but, if I want to spend a month on the top of a mountain in a resort, that can be arranged as well. I can also use special ports to come back to work on a daily basis if I choose."

Her eyes went even wider as she absorbed what he said. "Everyone can do that? Not just rich people? 'Cause wow!"

He laughed. "Not everyone. Obviously, if you are in a field that requires your presence, then you can't take off all the time. But this is normal in the business world, and it's common to port from one place to another this way. Go for lunch in Europe with a business partner or attend a meeting in South America in the afternoon. Time zones can be a bit of a problem though."

"I bet," she said with feeling. "And there must be currency issues."

"No, we now have a global currency and a global financial group that keeps track of the international monetary scene."

"That makes sense," she said slowly. "In my time, there was talk about doing something like that."

"It happened somewhere around the same time that English became the global language."

"Do you still have banks?"

"Financial centers, but you can access the same one all over the world. Makes traveling much easier."

"Do you have to pay to use ports?"

"Oh, yes, like the internet, we pay for usage. It's expensive, but nothing like plane traveling would have been in your time."

"That's a relief." She smiled up at him.

And damn if that simple movement of her lips didn't make his groin tighten. "First, you need to heal." He went to close the lid of the pod, letting her go back under. "Then we can explore. I want to show you a lot of things here. It really is a magical world."

"Wait." She pushed the pod lid back up. "Can you join me?"

"What?"

She gave him a slow sexy quirk of her lips. "Remember the last time?"

"Oh, God, yes, I do." He hesitated, hating that he felt like he needed to ask. What if she said no? "Are you sure? You need to rest."

"I believe we went over this once already. Sex in a healing pod helped in many ways."

Part of him wanted to correct her use of the word *sex*. It wasn't just sex for him. He didn't really want to know if it was only that for her. He hoped not, but this was not the time to discuss such things. Not if he wanted a chance to make love to her again.

She smiled, a warm, enticing smile that heated his blood. Damn, she was something.

He grabbed his shirt and tugged it over his head, tossing it to the far side of the room. "Make sure you miss the litter box," she whispered with a smirk.

"Ha. It's gone. Bet Charming didn't know that the rooms clean themselves."

And didn't that make her stare. "They what?"

"Absolutely. Housework is a thing of the past."

"My past, apparently." She reached out a hand and stroked down the front of his thighs, pausing before slowly climbing back upward.

His hips surged into her palm, willing her to explore further.

"Remember last time? You said I could have a turn?"

He'd barely thought of anything else. "Yes," he muttered, struggling to open his pants and to then step out of them. He finally managed to stand in front of her, his eyes watching her face as she studied him with a fat grin.

"So let's trade places." And she scrambled out of the pod to stand beside him. He was now fully nude, and she was fully dressed. And didn't his knees start knocking? He wanted this. Damn, he wanted this very much. He lay down on the warm bed, self-conscious for the first time as his erection stood tall and proud. He watched her watch him. He waited with bated breath as she reached out a hand and grasped him gently with one hand. He groaned softly and closed his eyes.

When he felt her wet tongue, he almost lost it. "You do that again, and it'll be all over before we've even started."

She gave a low throaty laugh. "Oh, I don't think so."

Chapter 12

S HE LOVED THAT he lay here so accepting. With all the problems she'd brought with her, he'd done his best to keep her safe. And now he trusted her like she'd never had anyone else trust her. And Lani wanted to make it good for him. For them both. She took her time stripping off her new clothes, loving the feel of his heated gaze, his appreciation. He had the ability to make her feel beautiful with just his eyes. When she pulled her midriff top over her head, finally as bare as him, he sat up and reached over to cup her breasts.

"Hey," she teased, "I thought this was my turn to run the show."

"Too late," he said thickly. "I can't wait. I need you now." He tugged her forward until she rested on top of him. "I swear I've been waiting for you forever."

Sliding his hands up to clasp her head gently, he pulled her down for a kiss.

And what a kiss it was. Fireworks and liquid heat fought for supremacy, lighting up nerve endings while melting her insides. Lord, he was a hell of a kisser. And she had to admit, an odd sense of homecoming was attached to this moment. As if she'd been waiting for him too. And didn't that train of thought take her down a direction she had not considered. He was here, and so was she. That was good enough for both of them right now. And she wanted him. She'd never been a one-night-stand type person and didn't plan on being one now.

Besides, he was her husband. And they'd yet to have a wedding night.

"Do you have a bedroom?" she murmured when she could.

"Of course." He reached up to clasp her head and tugged her down for more drugging kisses. She twisted sinuously against him, dragging her breasts from one side to the other, then flexing her hips and pressing her pelvis hard against him. He moaned, sliding his hands down to grab her hips and ground his pelvis up against her.

"You know that we could try out your bed one time."

He smiled beneath her lips before moving to trail kisses down her throat. "Next time."

She tilted her head back, letting her long blond hair fall down around them. "That's what you said last time."

He laughed and flipped her over to lie beneath him. She stared up at him in wide-eyed surprise when he came down on top of her, just where she wanted him.

She spread her legs, making a place for him. He settled in deeper. She arched beneath him, offering her breasts. He bent his head, tugging first the one, then the other, into his mouth and suckling. He stoked the fires until she twisted beneath him, crying out, "Liev, now."

"Not yet."

"Now." She wrapped her legs around his thighs and gripped him tightly. Then she wiggled beneath him.

He roared, lifted his hips, slid his hands down to hold her hips steady, and plunged deep.

She gasped at the invasion. At the fullness. At the rightness. Again. A tiny corner of her mind worried that it was dangerous to think that way, but the rest of her reveled in it. All her life she'd been trying to find her place. Trying to find her home in the world. Apparently she'd just been behind the times.

Liev lifted his hips, pulling back and back and …

She dug her nails into the smooth rounded muscles of his buttocks to stop him from slipping away from her completely.

He drove inside.

She wrapped her legs around him as he set up a rhythm that she was desperate to match and more frantic to increase. He picked up speed. Throwing her head back, she held on for the ride.

Inside, her blood heated as her body raced to the finish line.

She twisted her head, crying out as tiny explosions went off, but she wasn't quite there. He lowered his head and claimed her lips, his tongue slipping inside as he drove in one last time. His body stiffened above her, and he threw his head back, a long and low groan sliding out from deep in the back of his throat.

Then she wasn't aware of anything more as her own body exploded.

NICE. ACTUALLY A hell of a lot more than nice. Liev lay listening to the strong, steady beat of her heart. The pod started humming around them. The lid was still up. He wondered if it had the ability to take over and help even when it hadn't been closed. Then to his amazement, it dropped into place and set up healing rays all around them. He'd never heard of them being able to open and close on their own, but it didn't really surprise him. It was, in fact, very helpful.

Especially right now, when he couldn't possibly move.

"Wow." She sighed happily, her breathing only slightly calmer. "You are *soo* good at that."

He grinned, loving the lighthearted intimacy with her. He tugged her up close and closed his eyes. How had Milo known that this was what he needed? That he missed loving someone. Being part of a special twosome.

His kid brother was many things. Intuitive was the one thing he wasn't.

As Lani nestled closer, her leg sliding over his, he could feel her body settle into the gentle rhythm of sleep. That she could trust him after all that had happened made him feel good. He knew she'd had little choice over these major changes in her life, but he hadn't forced her into this step. And, although he needed her legally bound to him to keep her safe, she hadn't seemed to have a problem with that.

He twisted slightly so he could look down on her ash-blonde head. Who'd have thought she'd find a way into his heart?

He almost winced at the thought. He hadn't thought to find a partner anytime soon. He'd looked for one years ago and gave up when all the relationships seemed superficial and dull. He'd made what he thought were a lot of friends back as a young adult, but the friendships hadn't lasted, and the girlfriends had disappeared even faster.

He'd always been looking for something … more.

Dropping a kiss on Lani's head, he realized he might have just found it.

CHAPTER 13

L ANI WOKE UP, cozy and comfortable with the sound of surf breaking close to her head. Her eyes popped open to find Liev's decorating system still in place. She loved it. And she would so enjoy being part of his world with these types of perks. She pushed the pod open and sat up.

And laughed.

The sand was gone. Instead a long deck stretched from her pod out into what appeared to be water. She couldn't imagine it being real water, but Charming had apparently used the fake sand just fine, so who knew?

She tilted her head back to see blue sky and sunlight shining high above her head. This decorating stuff was incredible. She not only could see the surroundings but she could feel a gentle breeze and even smell the heavy blooms of the tropical flowers. She spread her arms and flopped backward in delight. "I love it here!"

"Ha. I wondered when you'd get around to saying that."

She laughed and rolled over to see Charming, walking gingerly along the deck, as if the water would reach up and grab him. He did so hate water. "You won't get wet, you know."

He glared at her. "What was wrong with the sand here? It was perfect."

"Ah, except I don't want the pod room to be your litter box. If I have to adapt, so do you."

"What can I say?" He hopped lightly onto her pod bed. "It was done in a weak moment. A nostalgic moment."

She shook her head. "As much as I can understand that ..."

"It's done, so forget about it." He head-butted her. "Think about loving me for a bit."

She stroked his beautiful fur. "As if I don't love you."

"Maybe, but it seems like you are loving Liev a little more."

"Not more than you!" She gasped in horror. "Never."

"Aha! So you do love him." He half fell, half sprawled on her.

She barely noticed his body landing on hers. Her mind was spinning with his words. And that *L* word. Did she love Liev? How could she? She didn't even know him. But she'd already acknowledged that she knew him better than her major asshole ex—and she'd loved him, or so she had thought.

Damn.

"Stop thinking so loud. You're disturbing my beauty sleep," Charming grumbled. "With all your activities, you might want to grab some shut-eye as well."

"Hey."

"If you're going to be kidnapped, you'll want to look your best. Just sayin'."

She bolted upright. "Why did you have to say that?" she wailed. "How am I supposed to rest now?"

"Seeing as how you forgot that you have bad guys chasing after you, I thought a reminder would be appropriate."

"Did you and Milo figure things out while I was resting?"

"*Resting?*" He turned his head and narrowed his gaze. "Is that what you call it?"

And damn if she didn't flush. "Hey, be nice."

He snorted and stretched out, showing his belly. She sighed and reached over to give him a little more love. "I wish I knew what was going on."

"Milo found out a bunch of stuff. Go check with him. And, while you're at it, we must have missed a mealtime in there somewhere."

"You wish."

"Hey, you satisfied your hunger. Now help satisfy one of mine."

Considering he'd been fixed before she ever got him, it seemed a reasonable request. Besides, she could feel her stomach starting to grumble too. "I'll see." She searched the island hut for her clothes, amazed to find them at odd places but fitting into the scenery, as if she truly were here. Once dressed, she stopped at the doorway for a final look and smiled. "Charming, this island look is perfect for us."

"Only if you bring back the sand."

"Not happening." She partially closed the door as she walked out. The hallway was still the same. She had to wonder why Liev didn't decorate the apartment as something more glamorous. Surely it could be a palace on the inside instead of this normal boring old apartment? In the kitchen she found the brothers, heads bent, studying something on the table.

No. It seemed to be the tabletop. What the heck? She hurried closer. It was another computer of some kind. "What is this?" she asked.

Milo lifted his head to stare at her, but his gaze appeared unfocused.

She switched her gaze to his brother. "Liev?"

"It's a new tracking system we've been working on for military applications." He grimaced. "Technically you're not cleared to see this."

"Oh, fun. The problem is, I already have." She sat down beside him on the bench and grinned when it widened to give them more space. "I do love the future, especially the decorating system you have in this place. Although why you haven't changed all the rest"—she waved her hand outward to encompass the kitchen—"I don't know."

"Milo doesn't like change. Or rather, we can't agree on a change that suits us both."

Milo turned to stare at him. "I'm not a kid anymore. If you want to redecorate, go for it."

"We tried it once. Remember?"

"Hey, you wanted the place to look like some creepy haunted house, and I wanted it to look like a science fiction flying ship." He shrugged. "So we did nothing."

Her jaw dropped. With difficulty, she managed to pull herself together. "You can do that?"

"Well, you have to pay for it, but the motto of to-day's world is that *Everything is available—for a price.*"

"Wow. Okay, things have really changed." She nodded to the table that wasn't a table. "Did you guys design this table too?"

Milo frowned. "Why would I care about designing furniture? That's so old hat. Anyone can do that."

"So this isn't a real table? You just designed the computer that sits on top of it?"

"Ah, you mean the fact that it's part of the table. Today, you can place computers on any kind of hard-ware."

Liev started manipulating his side of the 3-D image again.

"What are you looking for?" she asked him.

"The missing lawyer. She's the key to this mess. If we could talk to her ..." Liev trailed off.

Lani frowned. "Didn't Charming find her?"

"Yes, but she's dropped off the grid again. We tracked her until she just ... disappeared."

The big screen on the side wall opened up, and

Hahn appeared to step through. "Liev, are you receiving calls?"

Liev pushed back his chair and walked over. "Hahn. What did you find out?"

"There's no sign of Gina," he said nervously. "We've tried everywhere and got nothing. Her mother hasn't heard from her either." Hahn's face twisted as he said the last part.

Lani stood in view of the holoscreen.

Hahn turned to look at her. "I think the answer lies with your wife, Liev. Maybe if I could ask her some questions."

Liev immediately shook his head. "You can give me your questions, and I'll see about asking her, but Lani's not the problem. Gina is."

Milo nudged Lani off to the side. He lowered his head and whispered, "He can't see you here. If you stand in that square"—and he motioned to where she'd been on the floor—"he can see you."

"Oh, sorry. I didn't know." She lowered her voice. "Can he hear us too?"

"Only if you are in that box."

"Wow." She could imagine the technology being very helpful in many cases, but it sure seemed like an invasion of privacy to her. Or was it? Hahn had asked if Liev was receiving calls. Maybe that was the same as asking permission. "Does Gina live with her mother?"

Milo shrugged. "No idea."

"Maybe we should find out. After all, if she does,

and her mom hasn't heard from her, maybe something bad has happened to Gina. Maybe she didn't run off. Maybe she was punished for failing to grab me."

Milo cocked his head to the side, then reached into his back pocket and pulled out his weird fingerboard computer. After tapping on the silver machine for a few moments, he smiled and said, "She does live with her mother."

Liev, distracted by Milo, turned to look at them. "Does that matter?"

"Depends if she's in trouble with whoever she was to deliver Lani to. Chances are, failure is unacceptable."

Liev's jaw clenched. "Hahn, have you checked the hospitals for a woman fitting Gina's description, either dead or alive?"

"Oh, dear." Hahn's face twisted up.

Lani thought maybe it was because of the unpleasant media attention that his firm might receive if that were the case. Then her attitude toward all lawyers was awful since she had worked with Lawrence, the king of all asshole lawyers.

She sighed and tried to remind herself that Hahn was likely a very nice man. Just because Lawrence and Gina weren't didn't mean all lawyers were bad. Good ones had to be out there, right? She just hadn't met any. Except maybe Hahn. And the verdict was still out with him.

Milo shouted, "Yes! Found her."

Liev turned to face his brother, while Lani tried to

see what Milo's comp said. "She's in the morgue on Cronan Street."

"Morgue." Lani's stomach felt queasy again. Gina could have had an accident, but Lani couldn't quite believe it. She was afraid that these people were playing for keeps, and failure was not an option.

LIEV HATED THE look of fear on Lani's face. He pulled up the information Milo gave him and got into the databanks to give him a visual of the body. Sure enough, it was Gina. He showed the headshot to Hahn, watching the shock, the fear, then the lighting-fast calculation wash over his face as he tried to figure out the best way to play this.

"She must have had an accident. Although why they wouldn't have notified me, I don't know. Or her mother." At the mention of Gina's mother, Hahn's face twisted once more. "Her mother will be heartbroken."

Liev continued to read the file. "She came in with her tags missing and minimal clothing." That caused Hahn's eyebrows to shoot up.

"And showing signs of torture."

Silence.

Hahn exploded. "What the hell did she get herself involved in?"

"That's something I expect your help in finding out." Liev continued to read the file. "Her body was dumped outside the hospital."

Hahn dropped his gaze, but his shoulders shook. Lani didn't know if he was upset by the news or if he'd had a personal relationship with Gina and was affected on more levels than she'd first assumed. Regardless, finding out one of his employees had been murdered had to be difficult for anyone.

"Liev, I have to do damage control. Let me know when and if you find out anything else." Just like that, he blinked off.

Lani stared at the spot on the wall, wondering how long it would take before she got used to that.

"So much for his help." Liev shook his head. "Milo, can you get into the Council files to see if they have any further information?"

Milo walked over to the countertop and brought up the big 3-D unit and started clicking.

"Also didn't we find some of the bad guys' photos on the facial recognition program?" Lani asked. "Did that help at all?"

"We're running their list of known associates, trying to find out where they might be located."

"And then what?" Lani asked. "Do you have police you can call on for help?"

Milo shook his head so fast, his long mohawk looked to be in the middle of a major storm. "No. We've crossed the line. We have to handle this our-selves."

"And can you?" she asked, studying his face.

He looked at her, showing his inner wisdom and maturity. "We have to. A lot is at stake here."

She didn't know if he meant her or more but decided some information was better left unknown.

She felt helpless. They had so much to do. Normally she'd have made tea or coffee or pulled together a simple meal; yet it appeared at the moment that she couldn't even do the simplest of things.

She hated that.

She walked over to where Liev had gotten her water before. She placed her hand where he'd placed his and pushed slightly. Instantly a water fountain slid out from behind the wall. She grinned in delight. Now if only she'd watched how he'd made coffee. How hard could it be? Exploring the things she'd watched him do, she managed to open the cooler and to pull out some cheese for a sandwich. At least it would be a sandwich if she could figure out where the bread had gone. She remembered their first meal with a big chunk of cheese and meat. Back in the cooler, she found something that appeared to be meat. She pulled it out and turned to ask Liev about bread.

Instead, he stood in front of her with a large loaf in his hands.

She smiled and snatched it from his hands. "Next time, show me where you got it from." He tapped the counter in front of her, and a cupboard rose up. She grinned. "I do love all this cool technology."

Milo stopped what he was doing, looked at the

shelving, and glanced back at her. "What technology? That's a simple cupboard."

She shrugged. "It's more advanced than anything I've seen."

"Right." He gave a small headshake and returned to what he was doing.

She studied the cupboard, looking for other food that she'd recognize. Some were recognizable. Most were not. While the men went back to work, she busied herself opening packages and tasting food. One looked like crackers but tasted like cardboard. Another had brightly colored images of food all over the package but gave no clue as to what was inside. She read the instructions to find it was a synthetic supplement. Yuck. Must be something for Milo.

The bread was good though. She could really use a slice while she rummaged but couldn't even find a knife to cut it with. Finally, in frustration, she began systematically placing the palm of her hand on every surface she could find and giving a light push. Nothing happened for the first few tries, but she persisted and was delighted when she opened one cupboard, then another, and another. She investigated all the contents and realized the third one had a mother lode of utensils. She grabbed a knife and cut herself a slice of bread. She turned to study the cooler trying to remember how to open it. She pressed at various places but to no avail. The door would not open.

Ignoring the snickers from behind her, she said,

"Open." *Nothing happened.* "Open sesame."

Still nothing, but the laughter behind her grew. "Open, please."

Silently, the cooler opened. She turned and threw an accusing glare at the two snickering males and said, "You just programmed it to do that, didn't you?"

Milo nodded, a wide grin splitting his face. Liev walked over. He reached out a hand and hit a hidden spring. The cooler door closed.

"No, wait."

"Now you open it."

She reached out and touched the same place he did. It didn't work. She looked at him with a knowing glare.

"Again." He smiled. "A little harder this time."

Success. She grinned and reached in for butter. "What is this?" she asked about a big package wrapped in paper.

"Steaks for dinner."

"Oh, yum." She could really use a steak. "With baked potatoes and a salad?"

"If you like. Do you need more right now?" He motioned to the thick slice of bread she was eating.

"I'm fine, but Charming is hungry again."

Liev rolled his eyes. "Of course he is." He walked to a side cupboard. "I ordered this today. It's premium cat food."

"Oh, thank you." She watched him open some kind of odd package and pour a premeasured dose into a bowl. It didn't look like cat food, but it did smell like it.

It had an unmistakable smell, once you dealt with it more than once. Still, Charming should approve.

She hoped.

She walked back to the pod room, carrying a bowl for Charming, Liev following. "I love the South Pacific theme. It's stunning."

"I was hoping you'd like it. If you don't, we can always change it."

"Later," she smiled. "After I'm bored with the concept. If I ever get bored."

"My bedroom is a Swiss chalet."

"Really?"

He grinned. "Let's feed Charming and maybe I'll show you."

The look in his eyes sent a shaft of heat right to her toes. She murmured quietly, "I think I'd like that." She'd love to spend a private hour or so in his bedroom.

As they opened the door to the pod room, she gasped. Instead of her South Pacific island getaway, the room had been filled with cat trees and cat ledges, walking up and down the walls. Including a dozen cats apparently sleeping on various beds. Over all the scenic sounds was heard a deep rumble of a snoring cat.

"What the …?"

Liev laughed. "Hey, Charming, I don't suppose you were planning on sharing this meal with all your friends."

The snoring stopped. Charming raised his head, his nose sniffing the air. "Program revert."

While Lani watched in amused surprise, her pod room turned back to the South Pacific hut. "Wow."

Charming stood, stretched, and walked over to them. "I'm so weak," he moaned.

"Ha. Not so weak as to set yourself up right at home." Lani scooped him up and tried to cuddle him, but he wanted nothing to do with her. Instead, he scrambled out of her arms to land softly on the floor in front of his food bowl. He immediately burrowed his head into the food. Lani took a step back. "Amazing, Charming. You've picked up everything so fast."

He lifted his head and pinned her with a marble glare. "And why wouldn't I? Nothing here is hard to understand or learn."

She sighed. "Says you."

"It would be easy for you too. You just need to do things instinctively instead of overthinking everything." With that pronouncement, he returned to eating his meal.

"He's right, you know? Everything nowadays is meant to be intuitive and easier to do, minimizing time and effort."

She shook her head. "Then why is it we haven't sorted out who killed the lawyer and why she was after me?"

He winced. "That's a good point. Before I show you my place, instinct is prodding me to go see what Milo has found."

CHAPTER 14

WHILE LIEV WENT to check on Milo's progress, Lani stayed with Charming until he'd finished eating, then she bent to scoop his dish off the floor when the pod started to make weird sounds. It often made similar sounds when she was in it—but not like this. This one had a weird metronome sound to it. She called out. "Liev? Milo? The pod is making weird sounds."

In seconds, the two men rushed toward her. "It's probably nothing," Liev said. But his face said otherwise.

Milo circled it, his hands full of his gadgets. "Okay, this is not good. It's a tracking device." He pushed a button, and a weird *splat* sounded, like a power outage. "Not anymore."

Lani released her pent-up breath she hadn't been aware of holding. "Why didn't your bug finder pick this up earlier?"

"I think it was triggered after the first one was destroyed. Like a backup system. While it wasn't active, I couldn't have picked it up."

She didn't like the sound of that. "What if there's a

third bug that will start when it realizes this one stopped working?"

"It's possible but not likely. Still …" Milo attached the bug detector, its lights flashing to say it was working, right on top of the pod. "That will take care of anything else."

With that, he returned to his study of the pod, looking for the now-defunct bug. "I did tell Liev that the pod was dangerous."

The other two trailed behind him.

"You said a lot, but you didn't exactly leave me much choice," Liev snapped.

"And I, for one, am very appreciative of the pod," Lani added with feeling. "It's helped a lot. Though I can't say it feels very safe, and I'm not sure I want to sleep in here any longer."

Liev tugged her close. "You don't have to."

Milo rolled his eyes. "Can we stay on topic?"

"On topic, I just want to sleep," Charming said from behind them. "Who can rest with all that racket going on?" he grumbled.

"I thought you were eating," Liev said suspiciously.

"I was eating. Now I want to sle—"

A heavy pounding sounded at the front door.

"Milo, I thought stealth was on?" Liev ushered Lani into the pod room. "Stay here," he said to Lani and Charming. "Don't come out until one of us says so."

And he closed the door in her face. A final *snick* made her scoop up Charming and whisper, "That last part didn't sound very good."

"He locked us in." Charming stared at the closed door in shock. "That's bad. Like, really bad."

"Why is that?" She figured it couldn't be that hard to get out. It seemed like everything was either hand- or voice-controlled.

"Because the food is on the other side of that door." He turned until his flat face was pushed tight up against hers, his eyes round with horror. "We'll starve."

"MILO, FIND OUT who is here."

As usual, his brother was way ahead of him. Being naturally distrustful, Milo had set up multiple programs to keep the world out there—right where he wanted it. He valued his privacy. More than that, he detested the invasiveness of the government.

Liev walked toward the front door, when Milo said urgently, "Wait. It's one of the thugs from Gina's office."

Ah, shit. Liev froze. "Now what the hell are we going to do?"

"I don't know."

Liev shook his head, not happy with Milo's answer. "The Defino brothers shouldn't know that we are home. Stealth is on and active. No heat seeking, no audio, no power surges being registered. As far as the outside world is concerned, we are not home."

"Unless," Milo said, "they were the ones listening in on the bugs. Then, of course, they know that we are home. And, if that last device was a tracker, they'd have traced the pod here anyway."

Liev winced. "Then make sure stealth is on in the pod room, and let's see what this guy wants."

"Don't open the door," hissed Milo. "He might have come here to kill us."

That was a possibility as well. But Liev had other options. He opened the wall comp. "What do you want?"

"The girl," came a hard flat voice.

Liev closed his eyes. Damn.

"Give her up."

"Or else what?" Liev asked, deceptively calm. He stared at Milo, who was waving his hands in the air in a wild manner.

"She's nothing to you. But she's worth a lot of money to us. You already have money, and, with her, we will too."

Liev frowned. "That makes no sense. She is worth something to me. She's not worth any money to you. How could she be?" He managed to work just the right amount of helpless confusion into this voice.

"I'm not getting into an argument with you. I have orders."

"Orders from whom?" Liev watched as Milo finally stopped panicking and started calling someone—anyone—for help. He hoped Milo was calling the same people who hassled them all the time. It was only fair.

The big wall screen beside him opened up to show Milo sending a live feed of their visitor to the same department handling Gina's murder case. At the same time, Milo sent a feed from Gina's office showing the same Defino brother with her that morning that was here on their doorstep. Liev didn't know if any of this would happen fast enough, but, if the cops came, … he didn't want Lani anywhere around. Or Charming. And that damn pod needed to stay hidden.

Suddenly the male outside the door sneered. "Called the cops, have you? That's all right. You can't stay in there all the time. She's the one I want. Give her up, and I'll leave your freak of a brother alone."

A frightened squeak behind him said Milo had heard that bit.

Just as suddenly, their visitor disappeared.

Liev turned to Milo. "How long have we got before the police arrive?"

"They're almost here."

And, sure enough, the alarms sounded. Within minutes, a small force had arrived at the door.

Liev had to open up this time. He faced the officers, "Sorry, gentlemen. You just missed him."

"We need confirmation of the material that was sent to the department."

Of course they did. Resigning himself to a long couple of hours, he opened the door and let the men in. They had ComBots with them. Using combat robots was standard procedure when apprehending anyone considered dangerous. At least the authorities believed him about the thug. If that guy had had something to do with Gina's death, then he was very dangerous.

Liev immediately considered getting a ComBot as a security guard to help keep Lani safe, just in case he wasn't home.

He waited off to the side as Milo confirmed the video footage and explained via HoloKomp to the Council Security officials how he'd come into possession of the feed and why he hadn't turned it over earlier.

They all appeared satisfied with his explanation about not knowing about the dead woman until her partner called to see if she'd been in contact.

Just when he thought it was over, the person in charge handed over more orders. Both he and Milo were to appear in front of the Council.

Now.

CHAPTER 15

LANI HELD HER breath as she heard heavy footsteps approach. Other people were in the apartment besides the two brothers. It bothered her to be locked in the small room, but, at the same time, if the stealth mode meant what she thought it meant, no one would see this room either.

That should keep them safe. The pod itself was illegal, so even finding that would cause Liev big trouble. She was a whole new dimension of trouble for him.

She didn't want that for anyone. If anyone knew the truth about her, she'd never be allowed to stay with Milo and Liev. No, the best thing she could do was learn to blend in. To be one of them.

"Charming, is there anything that will help me learn how things work here?"

"Time?"

"We don't have time," she said urgently. "I need to fit in. I have this horrible feeling that Milo and Liev are in trouble."

Charming studied her, but his thoughts appeared to be far away. "There is no comp in here, is there?"

"I have no idea." She spun around. "Comp, turn

on."

Nothing.

Charming spoke up next. "Audio from the rest of the apartment *on*."

Immediately sounds of people moving through the rooms filled the air. Lani shuddered and squeezed Charming tight.

"We are to take you down to the Council right now."

"Why?" Liev asked. Lani shivered at the barely contained anger in his voice. "Why are we going back to the Council when we were just there?"

"More questions need to be answered."

Then Lani heard no more talking as they all filed out of the apartment.

Charming stared at Lani. "They've gone back to the Council without saying anything to us."

"They couldn't," she said absently. "He didn't dare speak to us."

"I will contact Milo then." And damn if Charming didn't hop up onto the pod and push some buttons on the unit that Milo had left humming away in the background.

"That's a bug finder. Not a comp."

Charming shot her a look. "They are all computers, and here all computers can communicate with each other."

"Oh." Of course they could. It seemed like everything here communicated with every other thing. The damn coffeemaker probably talked to the house alarm and vice versa. "So you can talk to Milo?"

"Of course. So can you."

"I'd like to talk to Liev."

"His comp is on Silent mode."

"Oh, but Milo's isn't?"

"His is never off. He's receiving my message now."

"Is that safe?"

"Probably."

She didn't like the sound of that. She also wished she could go outside and double-check that the apartment was empty. But what if it wasn't?

Then she heard it. The sound of a door opening. She couldn't help herself. She stared up at the ceiling as they heard audio of someone else entering the house.

Charming froze, his whiskers quivering.

He tapped the comp very gently, as if afraid that the very tiny *click*s could be heard. The unit in front of him flashed an answer back. He swallowed, looked at her, and said, "It's not the group who was just here. It's someone else."

She closed her eyes. "That can't be good."

"Milo says to not make a sound. Stealth is on, but …"

She grabbed Charming, the comp unit, and crawled underneath the pod.

She didn't know who the unknown visitor was, but nothing about this situation was good. "Did Milo say if they were on the way home?"

"They can't yet. He says he's sending help."

She thought about that. "I wonder what that means."

"No idea." He added slowly, "I wonder if they are bringing food."

LIEV GLARED AT the Council. "What was that question again?"

"We wish to know where you obtained copies of these videos." Off to the side, the videos of the two badass henchmen entering Gina's reception room were displayed.

"It's obvious where we got it. We do consulting security work for Hahn Driscoll's office." Liev didn't like where this was going. Sure, he and Milo had crossed the line by showing it to the police, but, as they were looking for a murderer, he hadn't thought they'd crossed the line that much. "Why is this an issue?"

"Because," the speaker said, anger putting an edge in his voice, "if you accessed the private feeds from the lawyer's office, what else might you have obtained and why?"

"Nothing other than the regular security feeds. Which is funneled to Hahn's primary security company." Liev tried to stay calm, but he was damn worried about Lani. "I don't understand what this has to do with anything."

"We have a murdered lawyer, who, prior to you sending this feed, is known to have spoken to your wife before her disappearance."

"No. My wife had nothing to do with this. As we've shown, Gina was still alive when we left. The conversation with those two men proves that."

"Except that, since both you and your brother are known to have exceptional skills with anything electronic, so you can't actually prove that you didn't doctor this feed." He pointed to the feed frozen on the wall, one henchmen's face stopped with his mouth open. "For all we know, this man was there visiting the lawyer earlier in the morning, and you just made it look like their visit was later."

"Good Lord. You actually think that we had something to do with Gina's murder?" His voice rose at the end. "That's preposterous."

"Why is that?"

Liev could hardly formulate an answer. How did one prove that he hadn't done something? "For one, I have an alibi. I've been home with my wife and my brother all day. Besides, what possible reason could I have for hurting Gina?"

"Gina?" This comes from one of the other Councilmen. "You have a personal relationship with her?"

"No." Liev shook his head. "No. I knew her early on as she joined Hahn's firm but not well."

"But she wanted to know you better? She might have pushed you. Hard. Became a little too pushy.

Maybe you told her to back off. Maybe she pushed back. You argued, … and things went from bad to worse."

Liev stared wordlessly at the four men staring down at him. He wanted to rage and scream at them for their blatant stupidity. "You have this all wrong."

"That's not what this man says."

Liev turned to stare, shocked as a very sober and sad-looking Hahn walked in. "Hahn? You're the one accusing me of hurting Gina?"

Hahn's dour face turned even more sober. "I didn't want to believe it, Liev."

"But you just can't help yourself." Liev's cynicism kicked in. "This is your attempt at damage control? Place the blame on my shoulders, then you and your firm don't have to take the fall for a rogue lawyer. Won't have to reassure all your clients that she didn't sell out all their secrets?"

Milo stared at Hahn. "Wow. Slick move. Of course, it won't work."

Hahn's gaze hardened. "And why is that, genius?"

"Because I'm pretty sure, if I were to access your office, we'd find a string of communications showing that Gina was alive after we left her office. *Your* office. The office you have full access to. The office you pay your primary security company to do whatever you want. The office where you can screen potential clients to do some of your dirty work."

Hahn's face became a picture of innocence. "I had

nothing to do with the death of my colleague." He managed to look outraged, yet grieving at the same time. "How dare you accuse me of such a heinous crime?"

"Oh, but it's okay for you to accuse us?" Liev was back to being stumped. At the same time, his mind raced in circles, looking for something, anything, the one thing that would get him off the hook. "Then let us take a look at your communications." He dared Hahn.

Hahn raised an eyebrow. "Of course. Here." And he dropped his comp onto the table in front of everyone. "I have nothing to hide."

Milo snatched it up, clicked a few buttons, and lifted his gaze to stare hard at Hahn. "It's a brand new phone."

"Yes, sorry. I lost my other one yesterday afternoon."

"Of course you did," Liev mocked. "Coincidental timing, I suppose."

Hahn stared at him blandly. "It still links to my office and home. Whatever."

Milo continued to *click* and *click*. Liev hoped he found something useful. His brother's head was bent like always when he was focusing on a new project. "Find anything, Milo?"

"Yeah, I did."

Hahn stiffened. "Impossible. There is nothing to find."

"Well, not on the phone. But I tracked it back to

the office."

Milo looked up with a smile and hit Play. Gina's voice could be heard easily. "You know very well why I'll be late for dinner." She sighed. "Dear boy, I need to meet someone. This is going to be an easy open-and-shut deal. No worries."

"Somehow, whenever you say that, it works out to be the opposite."

"Then come with me so I'm not alone. That way, we can go to dinner earlier, and that will make for an earlier playtime." On that last note, she dropped her tone, oozing a very low, suggestive sexuality.

Milo clicked on something, and the feed froze.

Liev said, "So, Hahn, would you care to change your story? After all, you are now the prime suspect. You spoke to her well after we did."

"That means nothing," he blustered. "And that conversation could have happened a while ago. In fact, I'm pretty sure that it did."

"Oh, I'm sure she was always wheeling and dealing with *someone*. However, by your own admission, this phone links to both your office and home, and it's a new phone, so you spoke to her after you got it. Which you said was late yesterday afternoon. So technically, you were the last one to speak with Gina."

Silence.

CHAPTER 16

L ANI CROUCHED LOW, making herself as small as she could. The South Pacific theme was open and empty. Kinda hard to hide here. She had no idea who walked the hallways outside the pod room, but, from the sound of the heavy footsteps and the pounding on the walls, no doubt someone was.

Her nerves were shot with every hard *thump* on the wall. The intruder was looking for her. She knew it deep inside. And the fear choked her. She couldn't take a breath. She clutched Charming so tightly to her chest, she doubted he could breathe either. She closed her eyes.

Thud. Thud. Thud.

She shuddered and buried her face into his fur. "Please keep us safe."

Thud.

They had to be following the signal from the tracker before it was fried. Charming shivered in her arms. She squeezed him tighter.

Then the door opened. She gasped silently and shrank lower.

"Bloody hell. Here it is. How the hell did they hide

this place?" The stranger walked in. From her position under the pod, she could only see his boots. Leather. Heavy. High. Studded. One of the Defino brothers. The boots were meant to instill fear. And they succeeded. She was terrified.

From the quivering flesh in her arms, she presumed that Charming felt the same.

The footsteps circled the room one way, then returned the other way. Back in front of the door, the boots stopped. "Damn." The boots shuffled slightly. As if he were standing in one place and looking the place over. "Who'd want a pod on an island? Stupid people."

His hands hit the floor, and he bent down to look under the pod.

And Charming attacked. He flew at the stranger, claws out, slashing and slashing, … and yowling.

"Holy shit. What the hell?"

Charming howled again and dashed away, only to come back and jump up again, this time going after the man's face. Footsteps sounded as the stranger—she thought it was the older thug—raced out of the room.

Charming gave chase.

A horrible alarm set off, filling the halls and making the walls rattle. Lani cried out and slapped her hands over her ears. "Oh, make it stop."

She scrambled out from under the pod, raced to close the door, and stopped. She couldn't leave Charming out there alone. He could be hurt. In danger. But the horrific noise was worse with the open door.

"Charming," she whispered. No way he'd hear her with that alarm going off.

Damn. She snuck into the kitchen, but she saw no sign of him. Scared to be too far away from the pod room, she snuck back and called for him again.

Still nothing.

On the floor, she found a comp unit. It wasn't one she recognized. She picked it up, wishing she understood how to use it. After tucking it into her pocket, she went to close the pod room door when she heard, "Hey, open up."

She pulled the door wide open. "Charming!"

He jumped into her arms. She shut the door with her hip and hugged him close. After a cuddle, Charming dug his claws into her arm. "Ow! What was that for?"

"You have the intruder's comp," he said, jumping from her arms to the top of the pod, whacking at her pocket. "I can see the corner of it. It has to be that comp. Let me see it."

Feeling ridiculous but willing, she laid it down on the slightly rounded top of the pod and held it steady for her cat to use. Boy, if any of her old friends could see her now, they'd lock her up in the loony bin. Then again, she would have been living there permanently after the last few days anyway if she tried to explain what had happened to her. "What are you trying to do?"

"See his connections."

She frowned. "As in, who he worked for?"

"And when he last had contact with that lady."

"Gina?" That might be helpful, but she wasn't sure how, since she was dead now. But, if they could find the person behind all this, she'd be happy. Maybe then she could settle in to learn about her new world. "Do you think the apartment is empty now?"

He shrugged. "I think so."

She walked back to the door and opened it. Everything was quiet. Maybe too quiet? She really wanted to make sure the damn intruder had closed the front door. All kinds of security was in place—but she was pretty sure the front door had to be closed for any of it to work.

Milo said he was sending someone to help them. Surely they'd be here by now?

Leaving Charming to work the phone awkwardly with his fat paws, she crept toward the front door. And stopped. A man approached the open doorway. Then she realized who it was. *Hahn.* Liev's lawyer. Still in his blue outfit.

"Thank heavens you're here," she exclaimed with a big smile. "The place was broken into. We've been trying to reach Liev and Milo and can't seem to get through."

"You did get through. The alarm on the place sent an automatic alert to them. That's why I'm here." He smiled with relief and held out his hand. "I'm so happy to find you safe. Hurry now. I'll take you to Liev."

"Oh." She was so happy to see someone she recognized. She raced toward him.

He was just outside the door. As she reached it, a clear shield of some kind came down between her and Hahn.

A look of sheer frustration washed over his face.

"What the …?" She reached out a hand but realized the shield had a charge of some kind. She'd get a shock. "Hahn, what do I do?"

"Shut it off from the inside." But the peculiar look on his face made her realize this was something she should know how to do.

"He changed it recently," she lied. "I don't know how. He never got a chance to show me the new system."

Anger swept over his face. He turned to look behind him. "You need to hurry, before someone comes."

She studied the wall beside her. She assumed another virtual comp was hidden in here with the controls she needed. But, even if she could open it up, there was no guarantee she could shut this down.

She needed Charming.

And didn't dare bring him out here where Hahn could see him.

"I can't figure this out."

"What the hell? How could he possibly want you when you haven't got even basic computer knowledge?"

His disgusted tone bothered her, but the building rage on his face bothered her more.

She stepped back. "You have no reason to speak to me like that. Our relationship is none of your damn business."

He glared at her.

And she realized this shield was all that stopped him from reaching through and grabbing her.

He wasn't here to help her at all.

He was here to kidnap her too.

LIEV OPENED HIS mouth to answer yet another question from the speaker of the Council. His own lawyer, Hahn, was now under suspicion. Hahn had excused himself, saying he'd be contacting his own lawyer. At that point, Liev had thought that he and Milo were in the clear. That they could go home. He'd been wrong.

His comp went off. He pulled it out, disregarding the frown on the Councilman's face. "Sorry, gentlemen. That's my house security system." He clicked through his signals. An alarm notice sent shock waves through his system. "My place has been broken into. I need to go. My wife is alone." He turned to Milo. "Move. Lani is in trouble."

Milo already headed to the door. Liev ran toward him. "Excuse us, gentlemen ..."

With Milo ahead, they raced to the portals. Liev barely made it into the same one as Milo. "Are they okay? Can you contact anyone? Lani? Charming?"

"I'm trying. But it's not as if either one is trained to override the lockdown system."

Shit. Liev winced. He hadn't done enough to help Lani. She was in a terrible position. And he'd made things even worse. Again.

His heart pounded in his chest. He could only hope they'd make it home in time.

The port opened, and the elevator closed. They were back home in seconds.

They raced around the corner, his breath caught in the back of his throat. He stumbled to a stop.

The front door was open.

And the blue shield was on.

Shit.

He came to a sliding stop, hitting the brakes just in time. "Damn it."

From behind him, Milo said, "I'm working on it."

"Work faster …" He tried to peer through the waves of blue electricity and thought he saw something. "Charming? Is that you?" He looked around to make sure no one else could hear him. "Milo, is that Charming sitting on the other side of the field?"

"Give me … one … more … second." A loud *click* sounded. "Got it."

The blue screen disappeared.

Liev rushed forward, over his threshold, into his entryway, surprised when he heard a new voice behind him.

"And now I've got you two. Better yet, I've got

her."

Liev came to a confused halt, looking behind him to find Hahn, just inside the threshold of his home, holding a laser gun to Milo's back. Milo, his comp still in his hand, had his arms up high over his head.

"Now, Liev, get the girl. I don't have much time."

"What is this all about, Hahn?"

"Did you hear me say, *I don't have much time*? I'm supposed to deliver her within the next fifteen minutes or the delivery will be late. Late does not cut it with these guys."

"Who?"

Hahn's face darkened. "No more talking. Get her, or I'll kill your brother. These guys mean business. Gina failed, and look what happened to her."

Liev turned his shocked gaze toward Milo, who stood helpless in front of him.

"Get her," Hahn repeated.

How could he? How could Liev hand over Lani? Yet he couldn't put his brother in danger.

"Tough choice, huh? Brother over lover? Too bad. It's not a choice. Hand her over, or you die too."

"He doesn't have to hand me over." Lani's cool voice drifted toward them. "However, I'd like to know who you are planning on delivering me to and why."

Hahn relaxed now that Lani was here with them. "I don't know. And it doesn't matter. They get whatever the hell they want."

Lani stepped past Liev. He reached out and grabbed

her. "Wait."

"No. There is no waiting, Liev. There is no choice." She tugged her arm free and walked toward the open front door.

Hahn grabbed her and shoved her ahead of him while keeping the gun still trained on Milo.

"Don't bother trying to follow me," he snapped. "You don't want to be where I'm going." Bitterness swept over his face. "Hell, I don't want to go there myself. But that bitch put me in the clinch now. So it's you or me …"

Liev stared, his mind racing to find something, … anything that would save the situation.

Hahn sidled up to the doorway, shoving Lani outside. With one last warning glance at the brothers, he backed up several steps into the doorway.

Charming—quiet and unassuming Charming—sprang into action, jumping high up on the wall and slamming a paw into the 3-D monitor. Instantly the electric screen flashed.

As Hahn crossed the threshold of the doorway, … as the electronic shield surrounded him, he was fried instantly.

The system flashed and sparked … and shorted out.

Milo raced past Liev, deeper into the living room, crying out in horror.

Liev could only stare.

"Jesus," Milo whispered, now at a standstill. "Charming, did you mean to do that?"

"Of course." He walked closer to what remained of Hahn's body. Charming proceeded cautiously, then caught a solid whiff and reared backward. "Oh, gross."

Liev skirted the remains on the floor and quickly disengaged the shield. Lani stared at him in horror from the other side.

"It's okay," he reassured her. "It's off."

She didn't look hysterical, but Liev wished she would be—then he wouldn't feel so bad about his own reaction. He shook uncontrollably. With a cry, she ran inside without looking at the floor and threw herself into his arms. "I was so scared. So scared," she whispered against his neck, squeezing him hard.

"So was I," he murmured, holding her tight against his chest. "Oh, God, Lani, so was I." He backed up, keeping her with him. "Let's get you into the back of the apartment and away from that."

"Gladly," she muttered.

He led her to a big comfy chair that shaped itself around her. "I have to deal with this first. Then you can tell us all about what happened."

"And we need to get something for Charming too." Charming jumped up on her lap just then, and she wrapped her arms around his furry body and cuddled him. "He's my hero today."

"He's everyone's hero. As soon as the police and those … remains are gone, we'll get him anything he wants."

"Food?" Charming poked his head up over Lani's

shoulder. "Food would be good."

"You got it, little guy. I might even be able to get that for you right now." Liev walked to the wall and opened up a cupboard full of cat food. "What do you want? Salmon, tuna, chicken ..."

"Anything," Charming said, "anything but ... barbecue!"

This concludes Book 2 of Broken Protocols: *Cat's Pajamas*.

Read the first chapter of Book 3 of Broken Protocols: *Cat's Cradle* below.

Broken Protocols: Cat's Cradle (Book #3)
Chapter 1

LANI SUMMERLAND BLACKBURN walked restlessly through the living room and kitchen. Her new life two centuries in the future had taken a strange and ugly turn. The problems besetting her since her arrival should have been over—instead things were likely to go from bad to horrible. Figures. Murphy's Law had somehow followed her to this time period. Like, how did that work?

She was desperate to calm the tension vibrating through her. The police had come and gone. As for the lawyer who'd tried to kidnap her, his remains had been removed. Life supposedly could now return to normal. Whatever that meant. She had no normal left. This time jump had come with no warning or preparation for what could happen next.

Life had hit her sideways, and she was still sliding. She'd done the best she could, and Liev had been a godsend. Then again, he'd been the reason she'd been plucked out of her nice happy little life into his—as a gift for him—compliments of his uber-brainy kid brother.

Since she'd first arrived, they had had nonstop trouble. From horrible pain to debilitating exhaustion to heated passion between her and Liev. That last part had been a bonus. But between that and the people coming after her, life had been a dangerous roller coaster.

And she needed off.

As they still hadn't gotten to the bottom of this nightmarish kidnapping scenario, they weren't safe yet. And, if anyone found out that the time-travel trick had resulted in her overgrown Persian cat now talking like a fluffy Einstein—and getting worse every day—would more people be after her and Charming? More than likely they'd both be locked up in a lab for the rest of their lives. That was so not going to happen.

Was it any wonder she needed a break from this stress?

Determinedly, she turned to face Liev. He sat, his chin propped up on his fingertips. Eyes closed, deep in thought. And she could just imagine what was going on in his incredible brain, one that matched his incredible body. Sex aside, Liev had turned out to be a hell of a good man. She walked closer.

"Are you okay?" She sat down beside him, happy when he opened his eyes and smiled. Something was still so weird knowing that this man was her husband. They'd only known each other a few short days. He'd married her to keep her safe; yet now she couldn't imagine life without him. Her cheeks heated as she remembered some of their best times together.

His gaze warmed. He cocked an eyebrow and murmured, "What are you thinking about?"

She gave a slow, intimate smile. "Good times." She paused, then added, "And I was wondering about …" She let the words trail off, not sure how to phrase it.

"What?" He reached out and slowly ran his fingertips up and down her arm. "If you need something, you only have to ask for it."

"I need to get away. From here. From all this nastiness."

He frowned and damned if a bit of fear, insecurity maybe, sat in the back of those deep purple eyes.

"Not from you." She reached out to stroke his cheek.

The shadow in his eyes lightened, and he sat back to study her.

"I was just thinking that I have a lot to learn. We need time together, yet people are after us."

He nodded. "All true."

"I was wondering if we could go away for a week or two. Where it might be safe for you to take me out and to show me life here. Where making a major gaffe won't attract much attention. Where we could spend a little time together. Where every move won't be watched. Where I can learn ports, and shopping, and …"

He held up a hand. "I get the idea."

"It's a great idea," Milo piped up. "We could all use the break."

Liev faced her, a question in his eyes. She gave a small laugh and nodded. Of course Milo could come. And no way would she go without Charming, her walking, talking miracle feline.

"A good idea as long as we all go," Charming said, as if reading her mind. "It's too dangerous for us to split up. Besides"—he hopped up on the back of the chair and butted his head against her shoulder—"who'd look after me?" His huge golden eyes stared at her in worry.

"Not going to happen." She stroked his silky back, leaning over to kiss the top of his head. "I wouldn't go anywhere without you."

"Or Milo," Liev said with a laugh. "It's a good idea. We both have a few things to take care of first, not to mention deciding on where to go. In theory, we could leave tomorrow."

She brightened. "Thank you. That would be perfect." She grinned, thinking about how easy that had been and added, "Besides, today is almost over."

Charming snorted. "What time are you on? It's barely after lunch." And he gasped, his eyes rounded into huge glowing marbles. "*Lunch*."

"No," Lani said. "You had lunch."

"But I had an early lunch, and that means it's snack time." He turned his flat face toward Liev and deepened his tone. "You did order treats for me too, right?"

"Wow." Lani rolled her eyes. "It's hard enough for

poor Liev to adjust to a talking cat without that same cat trying to order him around. Remember your manners."

"Ha. He's doing fine." Charming shot a leg into the air and proceeded to clean the back of it. "Soon he might even start obeying those orders."

She smiled and reached out a hand to stroke her four-year-old pet.

"Liev, as much as it's a good idea, I think we need to solve this problem first," Milo said. "The leads are hot right now. If we leave, these assholes will go under, and we might never catch them."

"I was actually thinking about sending you three away, and I'll stay here and deal with this," Liev answered.

"Oh no." Lani shook her head, Adding in a flat tone, "All of us or none of us."

He frowned. "Milo has a good point. This has to stop." He reached over to cover her hand. "If we leave, they'll just be waiting for us when we return."

"So we solve this first and then leave. Personally, I'm thinking a beach." Charming dropped and sprawled along the back of the couch. "I'd like some more sand."

Lani snorted. "Maybe you could just get a litter box instead." She exchanged a laughing look with Liev, remembering the last time Charming had come close to sand. "If that's the case," she said, returning to the problem, "what must we do to resolve this mess permanently? I hate the idea of always looking over my shoulder."

"It seems to have started with Johan. We need to find Johan and whoever was behind my lawyers' attempts to kidnap you. Hahn said that Gina had gotten him into this trouble, and *they* probably tortured Johan's name and location out of her. So we also have to find her killer. I'm hoping the two are the same man or group of men."

Johan was Liev's friend who lived in the top apartment—or used to. Lani had never met him. He was on the run from the authorities now. "Okay," she said. "That makes sense, but how do we do that?"

"That's my part," Milo said around the straw in his mouth, as he sucked up something bright green. "Finding them, in theory, is no problem, but stopping them is."

"Because we don't want to involve the authorities?" Lani asked.

"Partly, but they are involved already," Liev said. "Two dead lawyers cannot be glossed over." He reached out and tugged her into his lap. "We need you safe."

"I need all of us safe," she muttered, "but how?"

LIEV CUDDLED LANI close. He'd do anything to keep her from harm. Had already done several things he never believed he would have done. But they'd been necessary. "We're good at what we do. We'll find the

responsible parties." He squeezed her gently. "I promise."

When she looked up at him with those huge eyes
filled with uncertainty, he repeated, "I promise."

Milo came up behind him. "Sounds like it's time to
get back to work." He brought up the big countertop 3-
D monitor.

"I need treats first." Charming groaned. "I can't
help you until I regain my strength."

Lani laughed. "Ha." She nudged Charming's large
sprawling belly. "You're getting fat."

"I am not fat. Well, maybe a little, but I'm cuter
this way." He stretched out a right paw and offered the
underside of his belly for a scratch. When she obliged,
he moaned.

Liev shook his head. "He's something else. I'll put
on coffee and help Milo."

At the sound of coffee, Lani swung around so he
could get up. He laughed. "You are as bad as your cat.
Your treat is just in liquid form."

She stretched out on the space he'd vacated and
smiled. "In that case, we both deserve treats."

"Finally." Charming moaned, as if in major pain.
"Treats. I need treats."

Milo snorted. "How about a booster? Whoa! What
do we have here?"

Liev raced over.

Lani twisted to lean over the back of the chair.
"What did you find?"

"I'm not sure." Then Milo pinched his lips, and his hands moved faster and faster.

Liev stepped back and watched his brother work. It was rare to see him in the zone to this extent. His brother was sheer magic. And, when he was on the hunt, he was lethal. His hands flashed. The screens shifted too fast for his eye to see what they were. The monitor buzzed with the speed of the activity. It blurred in front of him. Then Milo made a slashing motion with his hand, and everything froze.

Lani made a strangled sound from behind them.

Liev could only imagine what she thought. Nothing even close to this in terms of home computing had existed in her time. Bigger, faster, and more complex computers were at his office, but not by much. By the very nature of Milo's genius, his baby brother needed tools available at all times. And typically the best that could be had. That meant building their own super-computers. Not a problem, but many of their inventions went way past computing. That's when they got into trouble with the Council and the cops.

Milo leaned closer.

Liev stepped in to look. "What is it?"

"An intersection of paths."

"Whose paths?"

Milo tapped the top of the screen, drawing Liev's gaze to the faces. Both Defino brothers' images sat on one side. On the other side sat the two dead lawyers, Gina and Hahn.

"So you've tracked all their paths?" Liev asked Milo.

"To this one spot." Milo tapped the monitor frozen in place. "At the old shipping docks."

Liev frowned. "That's the turf I'd expect from the Defino brothers but not the lawyers."

"Except," Lani interrupted, "Hahn said something about not liking where he was being forced to take me to." Lani walked closer to study the screen. "So maybe that's the headquarters. The boss man would be in a location like that, wouldn't he?"

"Only part-time," Liev said. "They'd have a home base somewhere a long way removed from that hellhole. Likely at the topmost end of the scale."

Her face fell. Then lit up again. "That would make sense. Could that be Johan? He lived pretty well in this building. You have no idea what he did for a living, but it sounds like it was just on the edge of legal."

Liev shrugged. "If we could track his path to the same area, then I'd say definitely. But as he's gone underground …"

"What about his known friends and associates?"

"He doesn't have any." Milo looked at his brother. "Does he?"

Liev looked from one to the other. "I don't know. I don't know him that well."

"Then maybe that's where we should start looking. Everyone in his circle. See where those paths intersect?"

Milo raised his eyebrows at Lani's suggestion. After a quick glance at Liev, he swept his hand back the other way, unfreezing the monitor. Immediately the screen loads flashed and sparkled as they moved at light speed.

Lani faced Liev. "I guess that means he's on the hunt again?"

Liev smiled. "Seems like it."

"So does that mean coffee and treats are back on the menu?"

With a smile at their tenacity, Liev walked over to the wall, where he started coffee. "I guess it does."

While he waited for it to finish, the house alarm went off. Lani gasped, her hand going to her chest. He reached out to her. "It's all right. We have company. That's all."

She took a deep and shaky breath. "Okay. I'll go back in the pod room then."

"You don't have to." He was already walking toward the door. "Not if you don't want to."

"Actually, I wouldn't mind." She gave him a wan smile, reminding him how tired she was. What she'd been through already today. "A short nap, with Charming, would be nice. I'm feeling *peaky*."

"Okay then." He watched her carry on down the hallway; Charming, somehow knowing what she was up to, followed close behind. Lani looked tired, melancholy. Taking her away from all this was a great idea. She'd only been here a few days, but they'd been brutal. The alarm went off again.

"Liev? Are you answering that?" Milo asked.

Giving his head a shake, he said, "I've got it."

At the door, he looked outside. Damn, another Council henchman. At least the suit and close-cropped hair denoted henchman. He could only see the back of the guy's head, since he appeared to be looking behind him, as if waiting for someone to join him. Not unexpected considering the break-in and death this morning. But Liev had hoped it would be over, at least for today. Like Lani, he was tired and fed up. The alarm sounded again.

Gritting his teeth at the visitor's arrogance to keep hitting the alarm, Liev went about accessing the security system. The alarm went off one more time. "I'm coming. You don't have to keep pressing the damn button."

Finally he unlocked it and pulled the door open. And stared in shock at the man standing in front of him.

Johan.

Book 3 is available now!

To find out more visit Dale Mayer's website.

https://geni.us/DMCRadleUniversal

Arsenic in the Azaleas

A new cozy mystery series from USA Today best-selling author Dale Mayer. Follow gardener and amateur sleuth Doreen Montgomery—and her amusing and mostly lovable cat, dog, and parrot—as they catch murderers and solve crimes in lovely Kelowna, British Columbia.

Riches to rags. … Controlling to chaos. … But murder … seriously?

After her ex-husband leaves her high and dry, former socialite Doreen Montgomery's chance at a new life comes in the form of her grandmother, Nan's, dilapidated old house in picturesque Kelowna … and the added job of caring for the animals Nan couldn't take into assisted living with her: Thaddeus, the loquacious African gray parrot with a ripe vocabulary, and his buddy, Goliath, a monster-size cat with an equally monstrous attitude.

It's the new start Doreen and her beloved basset hound, Mugs, desperately need. But, just as things start to look up for Doreen, Goliath the cat and Mugs the dog find a human finger in Nan's overrun garden.

And not just a finger. Once the police start digging, the rest of the body turns up and turns out to be connected to an old unsolved crime.

With her grandmother as the prime suspect, Doreen soon finds herself stumbling over clues and getting on Corporal Mack Moreau's last nerve, as she does her best to prove her beloved Nan innocent of murder.

Arsenic in the Azaleas is available now!
To find out more visit Dale Mayer's website.
https://geni.us/DMArsenicUniversal

Author's Note

Thank you for reading Cat's Pajamas! If you enjoyed my book, I'd appreciate it if you'd leave a review.

Dear reader,

I love to hear from readers, and you can contact me at my website: www.dalemayer.com or at my Facebook author page. To be informed of new releases and special offers, sign up for my newsletter or follow me on BookBub. And if you are interested in joining Dale Mayer's Reader Group, here is the Facebook sign up page.
http://geni.us/DaleMayerFBGroup

Cheers,
Dale Mayer

About the Author

Dale Mayer is a *USA Today* best-selling author, best known for her SEALs military romances, her Psychic Visions series, and her Lovely Lethal Garden cozy series. Her contemporary romances are raw and full of passion and emotion (Broken But … Mending, Hathaway House series). Her thrillers will keep you guessing (Kate Morgan, By Death series), and her romantic comedies will keep you giggling (*It's a Dog's Life*, a stand-alone novella; and the Broken Protocols series, starring Charming Marvin, the cat).

Dale honors the stories that come to her—and some of them are crazy, break all the rules and cross multiple genres!

To go with her fiction, she also writes nonfiction in many different fields, with books available on résumé writing, companion gardening, and the US mortgage system. All her books are available in print and ebook format.

Connect with Dale Mayer Online

Dale's Website – www.dalemayer.com
Twitter – @DaleMayer
Facebook Page – geni.us/DaleMayerFBFanPage
Facebook Group – geni.us/DaleMayerFBGroup
BookBub – geni.us/DaleMayerBookbub
Instagram – geni.us/DaleMayerInstagram
Goodreads – geni.us/DaleMayerGoodreads
Newsletter – geni.us/DaleNews

Also by Dale Mayer

Published Adult Books:

Hathaway House
Aaron, Book 1
Brock, Book 2
Cole, Book 3
Denton, Book 4
Elliot, Book 5
Finn, Book 6
Gregory, Book 7
Heath, Book 8
Iain, Book 9
Jaden, Book 10
Keith, Book 11

The K9 Files
Ethan, Book 1
Pierce, Book 2
Zane, Book 3
Blaze, Book 4
Lucas, Book 5
Parker, Book 6
Carter, Book 7
Weston, Book 8

Lovely Lethal Gardens

Arsenic in the Azaleas, Book 1

Bones in the Begonias, Book 2

Corpse in the Carnations, Book 3

Daggers in the Dahlias, Book 4

Evidence in the Echinacea, Book 5

Footprints in the Ferns, Book 6

Gun in the Gardenias, Book 7

Handcuffs in the Heather, Book 8

Ice Pick in the Ivy, Book 9

Psychic Vision Series

Tuesday's Child

Hide 'n Go Seek

Maddy's Floor

Garden of Sorrow

Knock Knock…

Rare Find

Eyes to the Soul

Now You See Her

Shattered

Into the Abyss

Seeds of Malice

Eye of the Falcon

Itsy-Bitsy Spider

Unmasked

Deep Beneath

From the Ashes

Stroke of Death

Psychic Visions Books 1–3

Psychic Visions Books 4–6
Psychic Visions Books 7–9

By Death Series
Touched by Death
Haunted by Death
Chilled by Death
By Death Books 1–3

Broken Protocols – Romantic Comedy Series
Cat's Meow
Cat's Pajamas
Cat's Cradle
Cat's Claus
Broken Protocols 1-4

Broken and... Mending
Skin
Scars
Scales (of Justice)
Broken but... Mending 1-3

Glory
Genesis
Tori
Celeste
Glory Trilogy

Biker Blues
Morgan: Biker Blues, Volume 1
Cash: Biker Blues, Volume 2

SEALs of Honor

Mason: SEALs of Honor, Book 1

Hawk: SEALs of Honor, Book 2

Dane: SEALs of Honor, Book 3

Swede: SEALs of Honor, Book 4

Shadow: SEALs of Honor, Book 5

Cooper: SEALs of Honor, Book 6

Markus: SEALs of Honor, Book 7

Evan: SEALs of Honor, Book 8

Mason's Wish: SEALs of Honor, Book 9

Chase: SEALs of Honor, Book 10

Brett: SEALs of Honor, Book 11

Devlin: SEALs of Honor, Book 12

Easton: SEALs of Honor, Book 13

Ryder: SEALs of Honor, Book 14

Macklin: SEALs of Honor, Book 15

Corey: SEALs of Honor, Book 16

Warrick: SEALs of Honor, Book 17

Tanner: SEALs of Honor, Book 18

Jackson: SEALs of Honor, Book 19

Kanen: SEALs of Honor, Book 20

Nelson: SEALs of Honor, Book 21

Taylor: SEALs of Honor, Book 22

Colton: SEALs of Honor, Book 23

Troy: SEALs of Honor, Book 24

SEALs of Honor, Books 1–3

SEALs of Honor, Books 4–6

SEALs of Honor, Books 7–10

SEALs of Honor, Books 11–13

Heroes for Hire, Books 13–15

SEALs of Steel
Badger: SEALs of Steel, Book 1
Erick: SEALs of Steel, Book 2
Cade: SEALs of Steel, Book 3
Talon: SEALs of Steel, Book 4
Laszlo: SEALs of Steel, Book 5
Geir: SEALs of Steel, Book 6
Jager: SEALs of Steel, Book 7
The Final Reveal: SEALs of Steel, Book 8
SEALs of Steel, Books 1–4
SEALs of Steel, Books 5–8
SEALs of Steel, Books 1–8

The Mavericks
Kerrick, Book 1
Griffin, Book 2
Jax, Book 3
Beau, Book 4
Asher, Book 5
Ryker, Book 6
Miles, Book 7
Nico, Book 8
Keane, Book 9
Lennox, Book 10
Gavin, Book 11
Shane, Book 12

Bullard's Battle Series
Ryland's Reach, Book 1

Cain's Cross, Book 2
Eton's Escape, Book 3
Garret's Gambit, Book 4
Kano's Keep, Book 5
Fallon's Flaw, Book 6
Quinn's Quest, Book 7
Bullard's Beauty, Book 8

Collections

Dare to Be You…
Dare to Love…
Dare to be Strong…
RomanceX3

Standalone Novellas

It's a Dog's Life
Riana's Revenge
Second Chances

Published Young Adult Books:

Family Blood Ties Series

Vampire in Denial
Vampire in Distress
Vampire in Design
Vampire in Deceit
Vampire in Defiance
Vampire in Conflict
Vampire in Chaos
Vampire in Crisis
Vampire in Control

Vampire in Charge
Family Blood Ties Set 1–3
Family Blood Ties Set 1–5
Family Blood Ties Set 4–6
Family Blood Ties Set 7–9
Sian's Solution, A Family Blood Ties Series Prequel
    Novelette

Design series
Dangerous Designs
Deadly Designs
Darkest Designs
Design Series Trilogy

Standalone
In Cassie's Corner
Gem Stone (a Gemma Stone Mystery)
Time Thieves

Published Non-Fiction Books:

Career Essentials
Career Essentials: The Résumé
Career Essentials: The Cover Letter
Career Essentials: The Interview
Career Essentials: 3 in 1